Mills

BEST SELLER ROMANCE

A chance to read and collect some of the best-loved novels
from Mills & Boon—the world's largest publisher of romantic
fiction.

Every month, three titles by favourite Mills & Boon authors
will be re-published in the *Best Seller Romance* series.

A list of other titles in the *Best Seller Romance* series can be
found at the end of this book.

Robyn Donald

DILEMMA IN PARADISE

MILLS & BOON LIMITED
15–16 BROOK'S MEWS
LONDON W1A 1DR

*First published in Great Britain 1978
by Mills & Boon Limited*

© Robyn Donald 1978

*Australian copyright 1978
Philippine copyright 1978
Reprinted 1978
This edition 1985*

ISBN 0 263 75056 6

*Set in Linotype Plantin 10 on 12 pt.
02–0385*

*Made and printed in Great Britain by
Richard Clay (The Chaucer Press) Ltd,
Bungay, Suffolk*

CHAPTER ONE

'HOLLYWOOD couldn't do better!' John murmured, well satisfied, into his fiancée's ear.

Tamsyn chuckled, then sighed, 'It really is too perfect to be true. A tropical moon, coconut palms, the sound of the sea——'

'—and mosquitoes!' A swift slap killed one of the predators, but John took her arm and steered her back towards the hotel, saying above her soft laughter, 'Yes, my darling, I know that you were sensible and used insect repellant, but I didn't, and I'm afraid that not even for romance am I going to be eaten alive. They'll probably give me malaria!'

'Fala'isi is not in the malaria zone,' Tamsyn told him demurely.

'Yellow fever?'

'No way. The worst you'll get is big red bumps tomorrow morning.'

He grinned, a white flash in the semi-darkness of the tropical night. 'Quite frankly, I'm nervous enough about meeting Grant Chapman as it is, without being handicapped by looking as if I've come down with a bad case of hives.'

'Nervous?' Tamsyn was surprised and showed it. 'But why, John? The company wouldn't have sent you if they hadn't thought you could cope with the set-up.'

'I know. It's not the work that worries me; without bragging, I know I can do the job. After all, I've worked on feasibility studies like this before, even if they have all been

5

back in New Zealand and not up here in the islands. It's the man.'

'Grant Chapman? Why on earth should he make you nervous?'

It was so unusual for her confident John to show signs of unease that she was quite bewildered. The firm thought very highly of their Mr Saunders, as Tamsyn, who was his secretary as well as his fiancée, knew, and although this survey was likely to be a little more tricky than most, because he would be dealing with Government as well as private enterprise, there could be no question of failure. Fala'isi needed industry to provide for the people, Grant Chapman was prepared to put up the money, and McHale's had been asked to provide the expertise. It was as simple as that.

'Why?' she asked again, stopping beside a frangipani bush to inhale the exquisite perfume from its waxy pink flowers.

'Oh—just that he has the reputation of being a very formidable person. Honest but tough. I looked over a profile of him before we left New Zealand, and he's an odd mixture. His grandfather was English—one of those upper class types who set out to carve himself a small empire in the Pacific instead of mouldering away as a second son in the family manor. He picked himself up a French wife—she's still alive, by the way—who came from the upper aristocracy. You know, poverty-stricken but very *ancien régime*. Fala'isi was almost depopulated by war and disease—measles, I believe—when he arrived here, but he saw his opportunity and took it.'

'He owned half the island at one time, didn't he?'

'Yes.' Absently John picked a blossom, held it for a moment, then dropped it. 'Sugar and pineapple plantations made his fortune. The son, our Chapman's father, was drowned with his wife and the old man died shortly afterwards, leaving Grant Chapman a baby, but owner of everything. Since then there's been independence, and the gradual handing over of quite a bit of the land to the Polynesians.'

Tamsyn nodded. None of this was news to her—McHale's research was always very thorough—but it seemed to ease some of John's worry to go over it with her.

'He has expanded into shipping,' she prompted. 'And tourism, too, like this hotel. I must say, John, that it is superb. Quietly luxurious with none of the brashness and vulgarity that mar a lot of tourist attractions.'

Moodily staring around the beautiful gardens, John said, 'That's the trouble in a way. He's a perfectionist. He doesn't want great scars over the hills and insists that the industrial complex fits in with the special way of life here.'

'Tricky,' Tamsyn said thoughtfully, understanding immediately. The way of life here seemed idyllic, a kind of lotus-eating existence where the Polynesians swam and fished and lazed the long afternoons away in their *fales*, sheltering from the fierce sun beneath high thatched roofs. 'He expects a lot, doesn't he? Industry and tourism don't usually mix, especially not in Eden.'

'We have to make it mix, darling. The natural beauty is not to be destroyed or commercialised.' He smiled again, bending to kiss her forehead swiftly. 'Never mind, love, I've just got a case of the jim-jams. Something tells me this is going to be no piece of cake.'

'What's he like?' she asked.

'Chapman? He's some man, almost a legend, and I'm not too sure that I'm going to be able to cope with him. He's not your usual industrialist who wants profits and looks

after his workers because it pays him to. He really cares
about these people, and he has immense prestige with them.
If he doesn't like what I come up with, he'll veto it, and I
don't need to tell you that McHale's will view that dimly.
We've got our Government very keen on the project, but
we're not the only firm in the running. Chapman is going to
be the man to please.'

Tamsyn squeezed his hand. 'You'll do it,' she said confidently.

'If I do—well, the sky's the limit for me afterwards.' He
gave a short, excited laugh, returning the pressure of her
fingers with more strength than he realised. 'McHale didn't
promise anything—that's not his way—but it was fairly
implicit in what he said that they've got a place lined up for
me at the top of the ladder.'

'Of course,' Tamsyn returned serenely. John's ambition
was an integral part of his personality; he would never be
happy to remain in an unspectacular position, however useful it was. At first this had worried her, for Tamsyn had not
reached her position by any such desire to excel. Indeed,
any less ambitious person it might have been hard to find.
Her dogged determination to do the job to the best of her
ability had been rewarded first by becoming John's secretary, and then, when love blossomed between them, his
fiancée. At first she had wondered if she should suggest a
change of work, but John divided his life very neatly into
compartments, and John the lover did not exist in the office.
There he was Mr Saunders, McHale's whizz-kid, and she
was content to have it so, for outside office hours he was an
interesting companion and a considerate lover.

The revelation he had just made gratified her exceed-
ingly, for never before had he revealed his innermost fears
to her. It seemed that their relationship had moved into a

new phase, if he was secure enough in her love to admit her into the secret parts of his heart.

So her voice was very tender as she slipped her hand into the crook of his elbow. 'You won't fail,' she murmured confidently.

'Let's go back. I can hear one of those damned mosquitoes homing in on me.' He laughed. 'I should tell Grant Chapman that his little paradise is not quite perfect, but I doubt if I'd have the nerve.'

As they paced back towards the lighted room of the hotel where the élite wined and dined and danced, she asked curiously, 'What's he like, John? As a man, not as an industrialist?'

He hesitated, an unusual thing for him, obviously choosing his words with care. 'Physically—well, superb is about the only word. Tall, dark and handsome, you can see his French heritage in his eyes and his features, but he's built like a Rugby forward. Not clumsy at all, in spite of his size—he moves like an athlete. If I were fanciful I'd liken him to a black panther—he has that kind of withdrawn arrogance that cats have, as though he doesn't give a damn for anyone's opinion.'

Tamsyn laughed, rather shaken by this summing up. 'You make him sound dangerous!'

'Oh, he is, dangerous as hell. You don't get where he is without making enemies, but you can tell he's clever enough to deal with anything that crops up.' He grinned, gave her a quick hug and resumed,

'Apparently he's a devil with the ladies; he's not married yet and he must be over thirty. That speaks for itself.'

'He doesn't sound very nice.' Tamsyn observed, aware of that pang of jealousy which always assailed her when she thought of anyone being 'a devil with the ladies'. John, too, had had quite a reputation before he met Tamsyn, and although she knew it was unworthy of her, she couldn't help that ignoble emotion.

'Nice? No, I don't think you could call him nice.'

John sounded amused, as well he might, Tamsyn thought. Her observation had been trite, to say the least.

'Never mind me,' she said, determinedly cheerful. 'I don't suppose he'll even notice me, so it won't matter if I do dislike him.'

'He'll notice you all right,' John touched a tendril of the silver-gilt hair that blew across his sleeve. 'You are beautiful enough to catch any man's eye; I'll have to keep a very stern eye on you, my darling.'

The teasing note in his voice made her laugh as they stepped from the warm darkness into the room. Some said that Tamsyn's laughter was the most attractive thing about her; certainly it was a rich, gay sound, the laughter of a happy woman with no fears to wake up to in the morning.

As she walked across to their table she was aware that she was being watched, and, as always, disliked the sensation. No fool, she knew that men's eyes lingered on her, but she had never got used to the feeling, perhaps because as a child she had been tall and lanky, with only her grace and the beauty of her hair and eyes to give her any attraction. When people stared one small part of her mind assumed that they were summing up her bad points. Unconsciously her shoulders squared. Like all women she was conscious of what she considered her bodily defects; those wide shoulders for one thing, and the fact that she stood tall in her stockings. Thank heavens John was six feet, and she could wear high heels without looking ludicrous!

The lights were not very bright, but they dazzled after the friendly dimness outside, and she was grateful when

John took her in his arms to dance. It would give her an opportunity to relax and let her eyes become accustomed to the light.

But after two steps John stiffened.

'What is it?' she asked quickly.

'Speak of the devil,' he murmured. 'He's over to our left with a party, and he's seen us. Yes—he's beckoning. Be nice to him, Tamsyn—I have a premonition about this job, and I'm sure I need all of the help I can get.'

As they walked towards the four people at the table Tamsyn knew with inexplicable certainty that the gaze she had felt on her before had come from Grant Chapman's eyes. They were narrowed in his handsome face, hawklike in their fierce regard as they assessed her.

A coldness in the pit of her stomach made her shiver. Almost she felt as if she was destined to hate this man. Some forgotten instinct rang danger signals in her brain, warning her to flee before it was too late, but John had not noticed that sudden shudder and how could she turn and run? There was no sanctuary for her here, nowhere she could run to, and her fear was completely unreasonable.

The two men at the table rose, the women looked their interest. Tamsyn knew that she and John made a striking couple, both tall, with their good looks and easy grace and confidence. Confidence! Never had she felt less sure of herself as John introduced her to Grant Chapman.

The touch of his hand almost made her flinch, but she had herself well in hand now, fighting down the ridiculous surge of emotion which could only be tension, because she knew how important this deal was for John. Like a naïve teenager she was dramatising a perfectly normal reaction, she told herself sternly.

The other people at the table were his grandmother, a

tiny wrinkled old lady who still possessed that indefinable chic of the Frenchwoman, a Miss Holland who was about twenty-five and very beautiful in an exotic, marble-skinned, raven-haired fashion, and an elderly man called Captain Marsh, very English, very upright in spite of his silver hair.

The introductions were formal. Grant Chapman had a deep, hard voice and a clipped English accent which contrasted effectively with John's New Zealand drawl; when he spoke his eyes were very hard and alert, moving from John to Tamsyn and back to John again. As Tamsyn sat down she felt that he had summed her up and found her wanting.

For a few rather stiff seconds it seemed that his grandmother, too, found Tamsyn not to her liking, but when she answered the older woman's polite enquiry about her reactions to Fala'isi with genuine enthusiasm a slight thaw set in.

'It is the first time you have visited the islands?' Mrs Chapman asked.

'Yes, but not the last, I hope. It's so beautiful—and warm! We're going into winter at home.'

Mrs Chapman smiled. 'You must not fall too deeply in love with Fala'isi, Miss Forsythe, or you will not wish to leave us. You have parents in New Zealand?'

Tamsyn nodded. 'Yes, I've just posted a letter off to tell them that we arrived safely. They don't fuss, but they do like to know.'

'As do all parents,' the older woman said drily. Something in the precise, barely accented tones warned Tamsyn that Mrs Chapman was directing a message to her grandson, but she refused to look his way. Miss Holland, whose name was Liz, hadn't taken her eyes off him, except for a few appraising glances at John, and Tamsyn certainly wasn't going to join her in such a public display of interest.

She could feel John's tension, tangible beside her, and turned, when her hostess's attention had been distracted by Captain Marsh, to smile reassuringly at him. He returned the smile, but it was more of a gesture than anything else, and not a meaningful one either, for his entire attention was given to Grant Chapman, who leaned back in his chair and surveyed them all as though they were completely transparent beings, all their desires and fears revealed to his omniscient glance.

Tamsyn felt her hackles rise. How dare he look so sardonically amused! Perhaps the strength of her dislike became apparent, for he looked directly at her, and smiled as his eyes challenged hers.

'Don't you like your wine, Miss Forsythe?'

With an effort she forced a smile. 'Why, yes, it's very pleasant.'

'You looked a little fierce, as though contemplating something distasteful. Perhaps you think that I'll spoil your evening by talking business to your fiancé? I never mix business with pleasure.'

Damn him! she thought frustratedly. What on earth was he up to, with his supercilious air of owning all creation?

Beside her John rushed into speech, sounding oddly youthful and brash. 'Tamsyn is quite used to business discussions and doesn't find them boring at all.'

This seemed to catch Liz Holland's attention. In a deep, husky voice she commented coolly, 'You have the ideal setup, haven't you? Nobody can complain when you take your secretary away on a business trip. Nice for you both!'

The implication was perfectly obvious, even when delivered with a slow smile which didn't reach her eyes.

John laughed, touching Tamsyn's hand in a gesture

which held pride and a certain proprietorial defiance.

'We are very conventional. Tamsyn on the third floor, me on the fourth. Our boss is a Puritan, and so are Tamsyn's parents.'

Mrs Chapman asked unexpectedly, 'Did your parents approve of this business trip, Miss Forsythe?'

Acutely conscious of Grant Chapman's enigmatic glance, and hating the conversation because it seemed to smirch their love, Tamsyn said quietly, 'My parents trust us both. They have no reason not to.'

There was an odd little silence, then the older woman said, 'I, also, would trust you, but nevertheless such a situation does not conform to the proprieties. Grant, I think that Miss Forsythe should stay with us while she is on the island.'

A dismayed Tamsyn opened her lips to object, met John's warning glance and said desperately, 'I don't think ...'

Grant Chapman's deep voice interrupted her smoothly.

'As you wish, Grand'mère. It should be more pleasant for Miss Forsythe if she is with us rather than immured in a hotel room, and no doubt she can fulfil her function as secretary just as well. Perhaps you would bring her with you tomorrow morning, Saunders, before we go out to the site.'

John was delighted at this unexpected turn of events.

'Of course, and'—turning gallantly to the diminutive woman across the table—'thank you, Madame.'

Another warning glance, sharp as a stiletto, made Tamsyn echo his thanks, miserably aware that she would get no help from him. Almost she could see into his astute brain; no doubt, in one way it would be an excellent thing for him to have her in the stronghold, as it were, but all she could think of was the tension of living in the same house as Grant Chapman, even if it was for only a few weeks. Blast Mrs Chapman and her outdated Continental outlook!

The husky-voiced Liz Holland wasn't too happy about the way things had turned out either. It didn't need the narrowed stare Tamsyn received to make her realise that. The disapproval in it was forceful, but nothing was said; apparently the elegant brunette was not prepared to protest.

Fortunately the Polynesian band struck up, the slow music entirely inappropriate, Tamsyn felt. Something fiery and Spanish-sounding would be a better expression of her emotions at that moment!

But then, horror of horrors, Grant Chapman asked her to dance, a note of mockery so clear in his tones that it was obvious he knew how she was feeling. John looked like the cat who had swallowed the canary. Wondering bitterly why he was so oblivious to Grant Chapman's supreme arrogance, Tamsyn allowed herself to be ushered on to the small, satin-smooth floor.

He held her firmly but not too close; after the initial stiffness had worn off Tamsyn owned that he was the best dancer she had ever partnered, and that was no disloyalty to John, who was excellent too, as she could see quite clearly, for he had, of course, asked Liz Holland. They appeared to be getting on like a house on fire.

'Liz has a great regard for the rights of an engaged woman,' Grant Chapman observed calmly.

Tamsyn flushed; lifting goaded eyes to his, she allowed herself one sparkling glance before her lashes dropped to hide her thoughts.

'I feel the same way,' he went on, that thread of sardonic amusement very evident in his voice. 'Which is why I'm not doing my best to sweep you off your feet. You're outrageously beautiful, and far too young to be let loose like this.'

'Thank you,' Tamsyn returned, her anger almost stifling her voice.

The arm which held her the right distance from him tightened, so that she was brought closer. 'You'll have to watch that temper, though. When you're angry your eyes gleam like a cat's in the night.'

'Mr Chapman——'

'Grant! If you're going to stay in my home you'll have to drop such a formal mode of address. I like your name ... Tamsyn.'

She looked up into eyes that were steel hard, cold as the Polar sea. A smile that was no more than a taunt curved the predatory line of his mouth, and Tamsyn felt sudden fear, all the more frightening for being unreasonable. Instant antipathy—just like that! Their eyes had met, and both had been aware of a flare of feeling, but instead of the attraction such instant recognition usually denoted, this was the exact opposite.

Tamsyn swallowed. 'If you would rather I didn't stay, I don't ... I mean, I won't be ...'

He let her flounder for a few moments before cutting in with bored decision, 'My home is quite big enough for the two of us. My grandmother appears to have taken a fancy to you and I indulge her in these things, making sure, of course, that she doesn't run any risk of being hurt or upset.'

The cold inflexibility of his voice made her shrink away as far as that bar of an arm could allow. His warning was quite definite and clear; Tamsyn knew that he was not making a threat he could not enforce. At least five other firms in New Zealand and Australia wanted this contract. If he cared to he could prevent McHale's from getting it, and he need give no reason. Oh, how she would like to slap her hand across those too handsome features, if only to see the astonishment which would follow such a drastic course of action! He affected her powerfully, made her want to seek release from the intensity of her feelings in something physical, but for John's sake and because she was loyal to McHale's, she would have to bear any hurtful insinuations he might make.

She didn't have to grin and bear them, however. Lifting her head proudly, she stated, 'I understand exactly what you mean, Mr Chapman.'

'Good, because my grandmother is very dear to me.' He smiled suddenly, his amusement giving him an attraction that had nothing to do with his hawkish good looks. 'That surprises you, that I should love my grandmother? I'm afraid you think me a monster.'

'No,' she answered, confused all over again. 'Enigmatic is the word I'd use.'

He considered this. 'A nice neutral word, meaning that you haven't yet got behind my social mask.'

'Do you have one?' she asked, greatly daring.

'Don't we all? You, for instance, look like a poised sophisticate, but behave as if you were just out of school. Yet I would hesitate to use the word ingenuous to describe you.'

And just what did that mean? Nothing complimentary, if the tone of his voice was anything to go by. Tamsyn decided to play it straight.

'I hope not,' she retorted tartly. 'You might as well call me naïve and be done with it.'

'Indeed?' There was an odd note in the deep voice, but before Tamsyn could pinpoint it he went on, 'Then I can assume that the schoolgirlish confusion of a few seconds ago was assumed.'

'Hardly,' Tamsyn returned coolly. 'I'm not in the habit of stuttering for the pleasure of it. If you don't want people to fluster all over you you shouldn't snap at them.'

'Ah, so you have claws,' he murmured, lifting one black brow at her. 'Better keep them sheathed, my child, before you forget that the satisfactory conclusion of your purpose on this island depends on my goodwill. And don't give me any bromide about not believing that I'd allow personalities to cloud the issue. Like all men, I can be swayed by my emotions.' He smiled unpleasantly down into her startled face. 'Who knows, you may find it in your best interests to hide that flaming antagonism. It won't be the last time that you have to be pleasant to someone you heartily dislike—for Saunders' sake.'

Was that another threat? Tamsyn didn't know, so she said the first thing that came into her head. 'You see too much, Mr Chapman. I'm sorry if you think I dislike you. How can I? I don't know you.'

'Well done,' he replied smoothly, 'but I'm not stupid, Tamsyn. Don't let it worry you, however. If you're a good little girl and keep my grandmother happy I'll try to forget that those beautiful green eyes sparkled with instant antagonism the moment they met mine.'

Tropical mornings were a symphony of magnificent colours, sounds and scents, but Tamsyn found it hard to extract any pleasure from the panorama from her window. Last night's events, starting with the arrival on the scene of Grant Chapman and culminating in what had come perilously close to a serious quarrel with John, were still far too fresh in her mind.

John had almost scorned her stumbling efforts to explain her aversion to staying with the Chapmans, saying with irritable patience, 'Tamsyn, don't come over all silly, *please*, darling. All right, so you don't like the man. Frankly, I'm glad—he's a sight too attractive for my peace of mind. I don't like him much either. That cynical arrogance grates on me as much as it does on you. But we have to keep him sweet, and if it means accepting his dear old granny's invitation, will that be so painful?'

How could she tell him that it was not so much dislike she felt for Grant Chapman, but fear? He would think she was mad. So she had had to remain dumb as he continued with a patience she knew was assumed.

'You'll enjoy yourself, sweetie. The old girl will probably bore you to screaming point with tales of her youth. But Grant Chapman is somebody, so you'll meet all sorts of interesting people. And he's given me licence to more or less run tame out there too, so it won't be as though we're separated.'

Then when she had still been upset at the idea, he had coaxed, 'You'll see how the other half live, Tamsyn. I believe the house is some place, a cross between a mansion in America's Deep South and a French villa on the Riviera.'

And when that hadn't worked he became angry. Her temper had fired, and for a few horrifying moments they had trembled on the brink of a quarrel; it was only averted by her capitulation. He had been sweet to her then, kissing her goodnight with tenderness but no passion, realising that she was exhausted and too emotionally strung up to return his ardour.

A frown creased the smooth skin of her forehead. Was that how it was always going to be, her surrender to his persuasion? Grant Chapman's cynical comment that it wouldn't be the last time she would have to suppress her emotions for John's advancement was only too clear in her mind. She could even remember the tight-lipped smile he had given her as he said it, the cool assessment in his glance.

With fingers that trembled she picked up her handbag. What on earth was the matter with her? It took effort of will to banish the lines and planes of his face from her mind. She was being utterly stupid to allow him to get under her skin like this! Perhaps it was the jet lag travellers spoke of, weakening her in some more subtle way than the physical. Whatever, she must overcome this unreasonable attitude, become the gay, confident creature who was the real Tamsyn Forsythe.

John greeted her with a hint of wariness in manner which vanished as soon as he realised that she was not going to repeat last night's emotional storm. Over breakfast he was laughing and tender, careful not to refer to last night directly. Tamsyn followed his lead.

The manager saw them off, saying that he hoped Miss Forsythe would enjoy her stay at Mr Chapman's home. It was quite obvious that their stock had gone up considerably!

She said as much as the hired car drew away from the kerb, adding, 'Did you tell him where I was going?'

'No. Chapman said he'd arrange things, remember. I suppose he rang up or sent a message in, or something.' John looked at her. 'Everything OK now?'

She touched his hand, moved by the troubled note in his voice. 'Yes. I must have been tired, I think.'

'Sure you were. So was I. It won't happen again.'

She laughed and shook her head at him. 'I think it probably will, John. I've yet to meet a couple who could say that they'd never exchanged a cross word.'

'I suppose not,' he said ruefully, then relaxed back

against the seat of the car. 'Never mind, love. This may not be exactly the way we'd planned things, but I've a feeling you won't regret it.'

'I hope not,' she returned, so softly that he didn't hear her.

The road to the plantation, as the Chapman place seemed to be called by everyone in Fala'isi, wound through some of the most superb scenery Tamsyn had ever seen, and coming from New Zealand, she thought that was some compliment!

As it was comparatively early in the day, the air was still cool enough to be comfortable, but the brilliant light made the sunglasses both Tamsyn and John sported necessary, and she was glad that she had tied her hair back in a bandanna, for the driver, a cheerful islander, who sang when he wasn't whistling, drove with his window down, one elbow stuck out at a rakish angle. Indeed, he seemed determined to help them enjoy their drive, pointing out especially beautiful spots with a cheerful disregard for any other road users. After a few miles Tamsyn became used to the fact that he drove with his gaze anywhere but ahead, just as she no longer jumped at the prolonged blast of the horn whenever he saw a pedestrian—and there were plenty of those.

This was not a warning signal, however. After each toot he waved, sometimes slowing down to call out a greeting or a quip to each grinning islander, explaining to his passengers exactly where in the family tree each person fitted. He was, Tamsyn decided, related to everyone on Fala'isi. Certainly everyone knew him!

The road was lined with villages and seething with people, pigs, dogs and chickens, all of them apparently convinced that they had the right of way, until the sound of the horn sent them scuttling to the side. Tamsyn felt the tight knot of foreboding centred below her ribs ease as she returned the cheerful smiles of the colourful villagers. Bright-eyed children giggled behind their hands, dignified matrons and grandmothers laughed and waved, and everywhere there were flowers and coconut palms and the vivid greens and blues of the lagoon seen through the trees.

Then the road turned away from the sea and climbed a mountain.

'Not a mountain,' John corrected her laughingly. 'Just a lava flow from the real mountains in the interior. It's steep enough, though.'

Banana plantations clung to the side of the slope, the palms almost overhanging the road, their big, shiny leaves reflecting the sun so that the car progressed through a kind of greenish-yellow haze. When the ground grew too steep for cultivation there was jungle, vine-tangled and mysterious, so dense that the sun was almost shut out. The driver pointed out breadfruit trees with large fruits looking somewhat like footballs, swerved to avoid a massive pig sleeping in the middle of the road, and broke into a song which required him to clap his hands frequently. It bore a relationship to the Maori music familiar to New Zealanders, but was gayer, with a more complicated rhythm. Tamsyn swallowed, hoping that the car was capable of driving itself.

Finally the vegetation thinned out, they reached the summit and he turned right round, announcing cheerfully 'Nearly there. The plantation starts soon.'

Tamsyn let out a deep breath and uncurled her fingers, exchanging a relieved smile with John. It had been a little difficult to respond to the beauty all around her, with every finger crossed! John, too, had sat tensely all the way up that lava flow, obviously itching to get behind the wheel himself, but now he too relaxed and began looking around with interest.

Within a few minutes they were back in the green light of the bananas. A few miles of this before the driver turned between two stone pillars on to a long drive which wound through plantations, then a garden, velvet-lawned, and planted with trees in informal drifts.

The house was built of white coral limestone, and bore no relationship to either a southern mansion or a Mediterranean villa! It was long and low and rambling on its knoll, looking down a long slope to the sea, almost modern in appearance, yet completely at home in its surroundings. Scarlet bougainvillea and another creeper with hugh pale blue flowers mingled against the walls, and Grant Chapman stood on the wide terrace, watching them.

CHAPTER TWO

THE sun drowsed down, hotter than most midsummer days at home. Apart from the muted roar of the waves on the barrier reef there was no sound on the breathless air. Tamsyn found that tiredness was weighting her eyelids, and understood why Mrs Chapman had banished her after lunch to her room, saying firmly that she always rested in the afternoon.

So far things hadn't been too bad. After their arrival Grant Chapman and John had disappeared into one of the rooms of the house and spent until lunchtime looking at the plans of the site while Madame, as Tamsyn couldn't help but think of her, entertained her guest in a small, daintily feminine room which must be a boudoir.

Lunch had been an informal meal on a terrace over-
looking the sea. In spite of the fact that she had felt the
impact of her host's glance on her more than she cared for,
it was a pleasant meal. Mrs Chapman revealed a tough
mind and a dry wit, and her grandson was an excellent host.
No siestas for him, though! He and John had left almost
immediately after the meal to inspect the site in person.

So Tamsyn had wandered around the luxurious room
allotted her, touching with gentle fingers the superb carved
furniture, and feeling rather insignificant in the midst of
such luxury. It was a lofty room, tile-floored, its white-
painted walls cool in spite of the heat. A bed stood on a
dais, four-postered to the ceiling, great swathes of mos-
quito netting looped back against the posts in pale green
folds. Sleeping in that would be like submerging yourself in
the sea, Tamsyn thought with a smile, but the netting
wasn't necessary, for every window and french door had
screens to keep out mosquitoes and other creepy-crawlies.

There was a superb mixture of traditions in the room;
the airy grace was French, the solid comfort English, while
the green and apricot ceramic tiles on the floor breathed
Moorish Spain. Exploration revealed a tiny bathroom
through a door in the wall; whoever had loved tiles enough
to choose them for the bedroom had had a wonderful time
there, for the whole room was jewel-bright with mosaics
arranged to depict clusters of the flowers of the island—
hibiscuses, frangipani, orchids and the exquisite bloom
which the islanders called *tiare aloka*, the flower of love,
with its deep crimson stars so lifelike that Tamsyn could
almost smell its heavy sensuous perfume.

Tall french doors led out on to a terrace, and here there
were more flowers, in pots and urns, climbing the wrought

ironwork to make deep pools of grateful shade where chairs and chaise-longues were arranged.

How the other half lives indeed! Picking up an exquisite jade water buffalo, Tamsyn stroked the smooth coldness of it. This place had been furnished over the years with taste and the complete disregard for expense that only the very rich could afford, and yet it breathed a welcome. Hospitality had soaked into the stone walls, she mused fancifully, for everywhere there were little touches which showed that Mrs Chapman had studied her comfort. A row of books in the bookshelf, the titles of the sort that might appeal to a young woman, the latest *Vogue* on the table by the deep armchair, scented skin-freshener pads in the bathroom, were all indications of a desire to please. One could be very happy here—if one's stomach didn't knot up at the thought of facing the man who owned all of this beauty and luxury!

Not bothering to stifle a sigh, Tamsyn sat down in the armchair and reached for the latest Paris fashions.

The plantation slept during the long hot hours of afternoon, but towards dusk it seemed as if a shot of adrenalin had been administered. There were footsteps in the passage outside, the distant sound of a car door slamming, masculine laughter. It did not need the tap on the door which heralded Mrs Chapman to tell Tamsyn that the master had arrived home.

'Very pretty,' her hostess observed. Herself dignified in black silk, she approved Tamsyn's appearance with a nod and a smile.

'You wear the colours of the moon—silver hair, green eyes and that pale fine skin—a splendid contrast to that man of the sun you are betrothed to.' A wry smile touched the old lips. 'You are surprised at my romantic fancy? All romance is now gone from my life, *ma petite*, but I still remember what it is to be young and trembling with the novelty of love.'

No sadness tinged the precise tones, but Tamsyn could not prevent the momentary compassion which shadowed her glance.

Her hostess chuckled. 'Each age has its compensations. It is a triteness, but true, nevertheless, as you will discover in your turn. Nothing is ever static, love changes, grief fades, even the passions at last leave us to peace. But I speak like an old woman, and you do not understand or believe me. I should not have done so at your age. Come, we shall go to the salon. Tonight there is no one but us, for I thought you might prefer a quiet evening.'

A quiet evening without John, for when they reached the large room Mrs Chapman called the salon, Grant explained coolly that John wished to work while everything was fresh in his mind.

Something like panic fought for expression in Tamsyn's face, but he was watching her closely and she hoped she managed to hide it.

'That means plenty of work for me tomorrow,' she returned lightly.

'You enjoy this work?' Mrs Chapman asked, allowing her grandson to seat her in an elegant Louis XV chair which was undoubtedly genuine.

'Yes, very much.'

'Even before you fell in love with M'sieur Saunders?'

Tamsyn laughed, accepting sherry from her host. 'Yes, even then.'

'When my grandmother was young, no girl of good family would have been allowed to sully her hands by accepting employment,' Grant remarked.

Mrs Chapman waved a thin hand in negation. 'One must

move with the times, and I think perhaps it is better, the modern way. We were guarded and cherished, but we were very foolish, reading poetry and hoping for a love all ecstasy and moonbeams! Young women nowadays are much more sensible, more practical, they do not expect so much of life and so are happier.'

'Do you agree with that?' Grant Chapman's eyes gleamed with sardonic amusement as he fired the question at Tamsyn.

She smiled. 'I have nothing to compare my feelings with. I'm happy.'

'You look to me as if you have always been happy,' Mrs Chapman said shrewdly. 'Even in those terrible years between twelve and eighteen.'

Tamsyn spread her fingers in guilty agreement. 'I'm afraid so,' she confessed. 'I had no reason not to be—my parents were very understanding and loving. I liked school and made many friends there.'

Her hostess laughed, her dark eyes appreciative.

'It is not to be wondered at. You have that which disposes people to look favourably on you, a most unfair charm combined with beauty. Grant possesses that charm also. You are unaware of yours, he scorns his and uses it only when it suits him to.'

Tamsyn smiled politely, wondering just where this charm was hidden; she had certainly seen no sign of it in Grant Chapman. Sexual magnetism, yes, but hardly charm!

'You embarrass Tamsyn,' he said now with irony. 'She's not used to elderly French ladies dissecting the secrets of her attraction. Any more and she'll blush like an adolescent, so turn those astute eyes of yours elsewhere.'

His grandmother chuckled but obeyed him, and there

were no more personal remarks from her. Instead they discussed a wide-ranging variety of topics which stretched
Tamsyn's conversational powers to the limit.

Dinner was earlier than normal, so Mrs Chapman told
her, but later than Tamsyn was used to. At home one ate
around seven in the evening; here it was an hour later, and
apparently when guests were expected it could be an hour
later than that, all to escape the heat of the day. The meal
was superb, a kind of Polynesian French cuisine, with sea-
food such as Tamsyn had never tasted before. Her comments led to an animated discussion on the best way to deal
with such delicacies as scallops and octopus, in which Grant
participated, much to Tamsyn's surprise. It appeared that
he had a Frenchman's attitude to the table; certainly the
wines were chosen carefully to complement the dishes.

After dinner Mrs Chapman ordered her to choose records
she enjoyed. Thankful that she didn't have to touch the
impressive stereo set, for Grant did the actual work, Tamsyn lost herself in the immense collection.

An hour or so later Mrs Chapman remarked,

'You have a refreshing wideness of taste, my child.
Please feel free to use this whenever you wish to.' She
turned her head to look out of the screened french doors.
'The light fishers are out. Go out to see them, Tamsyn; it is
a sight you should not miss.'

Out on the terrace a tiny breeze caressed her cheeks, but
it was still far too warm to need a wrap. Tamsyn made a
soft sound of wonder, for the lagoon was netted with lights
dancing in golden circles on the black waters. No moon
illuminated the darkness, yet after a few minutes her eyes
became accustomed to it, and she could make out the muted
white line where the great rollers met the encircling barrier

reef, and the fainter half circle of the beach, some hundreds of yards below them.

'They use rods or nets,' Grant said from beside her. 'The women get shellfish and seaweed from the reef at low tide, but this is men's work.'

'Are there many fish?'

It was an inane question, but she could not think of anything else to say, and to remain silent was definitely out! There was altogether too much intimacy in this warm darkness which cloaked them.

'An ocean of it. The islanders love bonito, which swims in schools, and have special boats for fishing it. Tourists go out for marlin and sailfish; they rarely fail to get one. On the other side of the island is a small tuna factory, one of our experiments. At the moment the Japanese hold most of the positions of authority there, but we hope to have islanders take complete control soon. They already man the tuna boats.'

Tamsyn watched as the lights re-arranged themselves on the smooth bosom of the lagoon. The only sound was the dull boom of the surf on the reef, a soft chant from the village down by the beach.

An exotic scent teased her nostrils. It was not frangipani, having more astringency to it, but at that moment she thought it the most beautiful perfume she had ever experienced. A vast and boundless content filled her being from an untraceable source within her.

Softly she murmured, 'It's so beautiful. No wonder the Europeans who discovered these islands thought they'd sailed into paradise!'

'They did their best to ruin it,' the man beside her returned grimly. 'Some things they couldn't help, of course—

Fala'isi was depopulated by an epidemic of measles, but many men made fortunes by exploiting the Pacific without regard for the people. Fortunately the Polynesians are a resilient lot. One can't blame them for being suspicious of outside offers of help, but life here is no longer fulfilling for the intelligent and progressive among them.'

'Which is the reason for the tuna factory and your project,' Tamsyn said thoughtfully.

'Yes. Most of the people are content with their life in the villages, but not all, and there must be avenues of advancement for them; the tricky thing is to provide them without ruining the way of life. The tourist complex has to be managed carefully so that their culture doesn't become debased by commercialism.'

Tamsyn nodded in the darkness. 'Changes must come, however.'

'Yes.' When the cynical note was absent from his voice it was extraordinarily attractive, deep and smooth.

'They have so much we've forgotten,' she said wistfully.

'The problem is to keep their way of life intact while urging them gently into the twentieth century.'

'A challenge.'

'Yes.' He bent, picked a pale blossom and held it for a moment in his lean fingers before dropping it. 'Fortunately I thrive on challenges. Are you cold?'

Tamsyn laughed. 'No, this is warmer than we ever get it. Even in summer our nights are cool enough to require a wrap, and it was getting very chilly when we left.'

'So Saunders said.'

The image of John seemed blurred in this seductive darkness. Tamsyn felt a sudden pang of shame, as though by being out here in the night with Grant Chapman she was being disloyal. With a quick movement she turned, but his hand fastened on her arm.

'Look—they're coming back in. In a moment you'll hear them singing.'

And sure enough the lights were converging on to the bay, drawing together like a swarm of fireflies. Tamsyn waited with held breath, listening for the sound of their singing above the thumping of her heart. It came, faint at first, then as they came closer to the shore a joyous paean of praise with the subtle harmonies which seemed instinctive to all Polynesians. The lamps flickered out as the canoes were beached. There was laughter and a deal of calling out, and then silence except for the eternal waves.

Tamsyn drew a deep breath. 'Do they do that every night?' she asked unsteadily, aware of strange emotions she had never before experienced struggling to make themselves felt. She seemed suddenly to be thrillingly, completely alive, every nerve stretched, every sense sharpened.

'Most nights,' he returned, and dropped his hand from her arm. 'Come, we'd better go back in, or you'll be dew-soaked, and Grand'mere will begin to wonder whether I've succumbed to the temptation to kiss you.'

His words tilted her precarious equilibrium, but she managed a laugh as they walked across the terrace towards the glowing square of light which was the french window.

'I doubt it,' she said huskily. 'Your grandmother strikes me as an astute woman.'

'She is, and being French she has a very down-to-earth attitude towards the relations between the sexes. Which, my dear girl, is why you are here. She doesn't trust that fiancé of yours.'

Anger stopped Tamsyn. 'Indeed?' she jerked out in a

tight hard voice. 'And I suppose she trusts you implicitly.'

He laughed, a low cynical sound totally without amusement.

'Not in the least, but by bringing you here she's placed you out of bounds. A man doesn't seduce a girl who's a guest in his house. Hadn't you realised? A *very* astute woman, my grandmother.'

'I think you're horrible,' Tamsyn said shakily.

'Do you?' He sounded amused and aloof at the same time, as though she were a temperamental child with bad manners. 'But you made that quite obvious last night.'

It almost sounded as though he was piqued by her attitude, yet he had made no bones about the fact that he had disliked her on sight. Tamsyn hesitated, thinking of John, miserably conscious that she had allowed her anger to take her over the edge of what was forgivable, but before she could say anything he cut in smoothly:

'Don't apologise. I prefer honesty to bootlicking. So if you're recalling what I said last night about allowing your attitude to influence my decision on this contract, don't. I'm a businessman, which means that I *don't* allow personal issues to cloud my judgment.'

'Then why—why——?'

'Because your antagonism irritated me.' He smiled in the darkness, then said with mockery, 'Smooth your ruffled feathers, and come on in. You're a nice little girl, Tamsyn, but your life so far hasn't prepared you to deal with people like me—for which you may be thankful.'

It was an enigmatic statement, but as he urged her towards the door while he was delivering it, Tamsyn couldn't query it. Later, as she prepared to go to bed, she realised that she didn't want to. He had relaxed for a while as they watched the light fishers, and she had enjoyed their conversation almost to the point of forgetting that strange antagonism which had sprung full grown to life at first sight of him, but he had very quickly reverted to type.

Could the reason he gave for his grandmother's invitation be true? Tamsyn could believe it, because in her own way the older woman seemed as worldly as her grandson, but she could not believe that Mrs Chapman thought so little of Grant's moral code that she could endeavour to forestall him by more or less putting Tamsyn under her protection. To do that would mean that Grant was a libertine, and he did not strike Tamsyn as being so lacking in discrimination. It would also mean that he desired her, and she could not believe that! That her beauty attracted men, she was well aware, but surely nobody could mistake whatever emotions were between them for attraction! And there was the lovely Liz Holland, who had managed last night to make it obvious that she held a very special place in Grant's life.

Tamsyn had read of antagonism as the forerunner of desire, but nothing in her life had ever made her believe in it. Romance was a progression from the initial attraction to friendship and thence, if all went well, to love. It had been so for her and for all of the couples she knew; if there was another path to love it was way outside her experience.

Aware of where her thoughts were leading her, and not happy at the odd feeling in the pit of her stomach when she thought of Grant Chapman loving anyone, she decided to worry no further about his remarks. He was probably trying to get some sort of rise out of her. Gloomily she had to admit that he had succeeded very well.

With a policy of strict non-involvement in the Chapmans' affairs she should be able to get by. After all, it would only be for a few weeks! Consultations with the

Government would take time, but surely even a government department couldn't spin things out much beyond a fortnight. And then she would be able to go back home and forget about Grant Chapman who looked like a handsome pirate and did funny things to her bones.

Unfortunately John was not nearly so hopeful.

'I'm sorry, darling, but I think this is going to be a siege,' he told her ruefully as they walked in the garden the next morning.

Tamsyn stroked the silken petal of a hibiscus, gold as the sun, with a deep-coloured throat like the heart of a ruby.

'It can't take too long, John, surely?'

He frowned. 'I'm afraid it can. Chapman is as fussy as the devil, so that means absolutely no mistakes. And this Government seems to be in his pocket. "You must consult with Mr Chapman",' he mimicked, trying for the thick Polynesian accent. 'Or else they say politely that they'll have to discuss this with their colleagues. Nobody will take any responsibility.'

'I suppose they have to be careful,' Tamsyn replied objectively, remembering Grant's remarks the night before. 'It's a big step for them, after all, and if it goes wrong it could affect society here for generations.'

'Whose side are you on?' he demanded half crossly. One hand pushed through his thick tawny-gold hair, a sure sign that he was bothered. 'It boils down to one thing—they want industries. Well, here am I trying to arrange one with them. They know that a fruit canning factory will help them immensely, so why all the fuss? The tuna outfit is doing fine.'

'Mr Chapman said it's a small affair, more or less a try-out,' Tamsyn murmured.

'Has he been discussing this with you?'

'Hardly. He gave a sort of résumé of his requirements for the place.'

'Tell me exactly what he said,' he demanded eagerly.

It was easy enough. Tamsyn felt that every word Grant Chapman had said to her was engraved on her brain. When she had finished John commented wearily:

'Cagey devil. There's nothing new in that, but I don't suppose he's got where he is by chatting to secretaries.' His quick hug robbed the words of any sting. 'Ah well, I'll have to plod on, I suppose. Everything OK?'

'Yes, of course.'

'Then I'll be on my way. I'll see you tonight, darling.'

The morning passed quickly. Tamsyn arranged John's notes in order, typed a set of rough estimates he had made and several letters. A wide table had been put into a corner of her bedroom to act as a desk. Leaving it bare except for the typewriter, she made her way to the hall, wondering just how one got letters posted here.

A maid was dusting, humming softly to herself as she worked. As Tamsyn came through the entrance she looked up and smiled, superb teeth flashing.

'Good morning,' said Tamsyn, smiling in turn. 'Can you tell me where to put these letters so that they'll catch the post?'

'Here,' the girl said, holding up a wide bowl of some black wood, bound with silver.

A voice from behind made both of them turn. 'They can go with mine,' said Grant Chapman. 'Have you stamps?'

'No.'

'Come into the office and I'll get you some.'

The office was a big room, lined with bookshelves; another room opened off it where Tamsyn caught a glimpse of filing cabinets and heard the quiet click of an electric typewriter.

At the pressing of a button a man came through, a middle-aged slightly stooped Englishman who was introduced as Steven Tolman. He greeted Tamsyn pleasantly, without curiosity, and promised to send the letters off when he took Grant's into town later that day.

'I'll get you stamps,' he said. 'Just bring any correspondence you want to get away and I'll see that it goes.'

'Thank you very much,' said Tamsyn. 'But there's no need, my boss will be able to get them off.'

'It's no bother.' He seemed to mean it, so she handed over the mail, and allowed herself to be shown out by Grant Chapman.

'Finished for the day?' he asked aloofly.

'So far.'

'Care to swim?'

Her astonishment must have shown in her expression, because he smiled mockingly. 'The climate here is conducive to spending a lot of time in the water. I'll meet you on the terrace in ten minutes. Don't bother to change.'

The pool was reached by walking down a flagged path beneath a pergola draped with what seemed to be white, pink and scarlet jasmine. The scent was erotically heavy, almost stiffling.

'Quisqualis,' Grant Chapman murmured, noticing the interest with which Tamsyn looked at it. 'I believe it's also called Rangoon creeper.'

'It's beautiful,' she replied, adding half wistfully, 'All of this would make my mother enormously excited. She's an ardent gardener, and would be so envious of the hibiscuses. We can grow them well, but they stop flowering about now.'

'They never stop here,' he commented. 'I liked Auckland—all of New Zealand, for that matter.'

'Have you visited it often?'

He nodded, a stray beam of sunlight striking fire from his hair. 'Quite frequently. I have business interests there, and friends. Where do your parents live?'

'In a little town fifty miles north of Auckland. Dad owns a dairy farm, he breeds pedigree Jerseys. My older brother is working for him. Eventually he'll take over the farm and Mum and Dad will retire to a cottage they have at one of the beaches near there.'

'Any other family?' he asked idly.

'A little sister—their late apple. Sarah is ten.'

She stopped, sure that any more family details would bore him, but he asked, 'Does she look like you?'

'No, she's a fiery redhead, with a riotous mass of curls. She had the family green eyes, though, and hates them.'

He touched the cap of shining silver by his shoulder.

'Yours is beautiful—a gilt helmet. Why do you wear it so short?'

Oddly shaken by the intimacy of the gesture, for his voice was cool, she shrugged. 'It gets too wispy if I grow it. Fine hair is a nuisance.'

'Pleasant to touch, or run your fingers through, as no doubt Saunders tells you,' he said with a sharp smile.

Tamsyn bit her lip, but fortunately the pool opened out before them and she was spared the necessity of trying to find some sort of answer.

It was beautiful. At one end a fountain rose into the warm air like a spire of crystal, shimmering with its own rainbow. Down each side of the incredibly blue pool were pillars supporting a pergola draped with creepers of blue and gold; in the restful shade were chairs and loungers and tables. A little Greek temple faced them, white and gleaming in the sun, a delicious fake and yet not inappropriate.

'Chapman's Folly,' the man beside her said drily. 'A whim of my grandfather's.'

'I love it,' Tamsyn replied, warmly appreciative.

'One gets used to it.'

She felt rebuffed by the cool deliberation of his voice. Fake Greek it might be externally, but there was no mistaking the luxury inside.

Tamsyn changed into her bathing suit in a cubicle, one wall of which was mirror, and stood for a moment looking at herself. Thank heavens she had brought a one-piece costume! There was no way that she was going to wear a bikini while Grant Chapman was around to look her over with those coldly insolent eyes. Not that this could be called anything but revealing, for it was almost exactly the same colour as the remnants of her summer tan and fitted like a second skin, but at least it covered her decently— except for the fact that it was completely backless! She surveyed the expanse of skin over one shoulder, then shrugged. Blow him! She had worn it on the beaches of New Zealand and not worried one iota about it, and she was not going to let one man make her feel selfconscious. That would make him far too important.

But it was with the feeling that she was removing some form of protection that she slipped her engagement ring into her bag, and when she went out into the sun she dived into the water without looking around, setting off for the fountain with a powerful crawl.

The water was like silk against her skin, far warmer than any she had ever swum in, so that the cool shower from the fountain came as a surprise. She trod water watching Grant as he cut through the water like an Olympic finalist.

Peevishly deciding that he probably did everything superbly well, she resolutely switched her attention and began to play, enjoying with a lightened heart the complete freedom and weightlessness.

He didn't come near her, apparently quite happy to continue his workout with no distractions. Tamsyn told herself that she was glad, and spent much time around the fountain, loving the novelty of swimming through its spray.

When he appeared beside her she made an instinctive startled movement away from him, afraid of—what? His masculinity? In trunks he was big and lithe and very dark, burned with a bone deep tan. Beneath the shiny veil of water, muscles rippled as he caught her hand.

'You'd better get out—this sun is a lot fiercer than any you're used to.'

She nodded, something blocking her throat so that she could not speak, and turned blindly for the side. But he did not let her go. A flame gleaming in the dark eyes he pulled her into the circle of his arms and kissed her unresisting lips.

Something happened, something wild and fierce and totally unlike anything that had ever occurred to Tamsyn before. The fountain sprinkled her shoulders and face, but she was unaware of it, just as she was unaware that her feet left the bottom of the pool. She did not move, but her body melted and became animated by a yearning so fierce that she could think of nothing but the hardness of Grant against her, the coolness of his lips, the rise and fall of his chest as it crushed her breasts.

When he let her go she opened her eyes and looked at him, her green eyes grave and questioning.

'I'm not going to apologise,' he murmured. 'You are beautiful and that's excuse enough.'

As if to give emphasis to his words she found that Liz Holland was there for lunch, very svelte and subtly proprietorial, her husky voice softening when she spoke to Grant. Tamsyn forced herself to act normally, fiercely determined that he should not think one kiss had affected her in any way. Apparently they were going out after lunch; it seemed that neither Grant nor Liz bothered about the siesta habit. They were going to a beach somewhere with friends.

Back in her room Tamsyn roamed restlessly, trying to look objectively at those few seconds out of time. It should have been easy to rationalise the whole thing; after all, what had really happened? A man had succumbed to the temptation to kiss a woman. There had been no passion in that brief embrace. Indeed, it had been almost impersonal, except for the cataclysmic effect it had had on her.

So, she told herself sternly, you've discovered something. Even when in love, a woman can feel desire for another man. Did it matter very much? She was bound to John by ties far stronger than mere physical attraction, ties of love and respect, shared memories of laughter and passion and the self-control they had imposed on themselves. It would have been easy to surrender to their need for each other, but they had not done so, had never even discussed the matter, which proved, surely, that their love was blessed by that empathy which comes when two hearts are truly sympathetic.

The question of whether to tell John gnawed at her mind. Not to tell him seemed to give the foolish incident an importance it did not warrant, but John was so worried about his project that she hated to add to his cares. After all, it *was* unimportant—there could be no doubt about that! And John had an odd attitude towards this job;

almost fey, as though he was expecting trouble all along the
way. If he was upset he would probably demand that she
come back to the hotel: he was not normally jealous, but no
man would be happy if his fiancée had been kissed by a
complete stranger. And if he did react like that it would
sour relations between him and Grant Chapman.

Tamsyn pressed fingers to her aching temples. Grant had
said that he did not allow personal affairs to cloud his
judgment, but it would make things so much more difficult
for John if he resented the man he had to work with.

At last, staring at the muted tones of the tiled floor, she
came to her decision. Although it would be the first time she
had ever kept a secret from John she would wait until this
whole business was over and they were safely back in New
Zealand before she told him. That way she would not be
disloyal to their love, but there would be no further cares
for him to cope with. It would not be pleasant to hide a
secret, but it would only be for a short time, please God.

CHAPTER THREE

TRAITORS, Tamsyn decided, must have a most uncom-
fortable life. Her decision was made, but it spite of all of
the arguments in favour of it she could not prevent herself
from feeling guilty, and the temptation to confess to John
and cleanse herself almost overcame her in the evening as
they chatted quietly together on the terrace. Grant and Liz
Holland were dancing to a record. Mrs Chapman, or Madame, as Tamsyn called her, to her great pleasure, was talking with a couple of her own age who were guests for the

evening, and John had steered her out on to the terrace.

'We'd better stand in the light,' he commented lightly. 'Your hostess has a distinctly chaperonish glint in her eye!'

But once outside, the gaiety he had shown all evening fell away from him like a cloak donned for the occasion. A small frown drew Tamsyn's brows together as he stared moodily out into the velvet darkness, rasping a hand down the side of his face.

'Tired?' she asked softly.

'Bushed. There's a stack of work for you to get through tomorrow. I've spent the day going from government department to government department, and the only thing I've learned is that our biggest rivals are an Australian firm, Smythe, Smythe and Sons.'

'I've heard of them, of course.'

'Yes, they're big, much bigger than us. Apparently—or as far as I could make out—there seems to be some feeling that a big firm would have advantages we haven't.' His fist clenched on the balustrading. 'Tam, this is the most important thing I've ever had to deal with. McHale expects me to bring home the bacon and I must, or feel humiliated.'

'But, darling——'

'*Humiliated*,' he reiterated savagely. 'It's that important to me. If only I knew which way Chapman leans! He'll have the casting vote, blast him.'

Turning, he cast a glowering look at the tall figure of their host. 'Look at him, smiling down at her as though he hasn't a care in the world. I feel I could hate him!'

Devoutly thankful that she hadn't told him about the kiss, Tamsyn said quietly, 'John, you're allowing yourself to get too het-up about this. It's not like you, my darling.'

'Oh—I know.' A sound that was almost a groan broke from him. 'This thing is really getting me down and I can't explain why! I've had a thing about it right from the start—which you don't need to tell me is absolutely ridiculous. Hell, I've done my best to talk myself out of this state of mind, but I just seem to reinforce the foreboding.'

Tamsyn touched his arm, worried by the note of despair in his normally confident voice. This mood was so unlike John that she had no idea how to cope with it. Never before had his ambition ridden him to the extent of undermining his self-confidence. Never before had he been so personally concerned with getting a contract that its loss would be a humiliation!

On the verge of offering what could only be soothing platitudes she reconsidered and wisely kept her mouth firmly closed. Though her heart ached for him there was nothing that she could do. If they had been married he could have had the temporary solace of her body, but as things were, he was denied even the pleasure of the sort of lovemaking they enjoyed together. Madame was watching.

An hysterical bubble of laughter threatened to burst from her. As John had said, this whole situation was ridiculous, but there seemed no way of extricating themselves from it.

'Is there anything I can do?' she asked gravely, mastering her desire to laugh.

'You can keep him sweet,' he returned, casting a quick fierce glance at their host. 'He's too clever to give anything away.' He hesitated, his eyes hard, almost as though making a decision.

In the silence that followed the finish of the record Liz Holland's husky voice sounded, gay and provocative. John turned and stared out to sea again, obviously thinking deeply, his brow furrowed, but the expression of anguish clearing from his face.

Tamsyn waited. After a few minutes he said softly, 'I know we can give him a good deal. So can Smythe, Smythe & Sons, blast them. As I see it, the one who wins will be the one who produces a scheme which takes those scruples of his most into account. Which means that that's the angle we have to stress in our report. Tomorrow I'll ring for an anthropologist; someone who's made a study of Polynesian cultures. I daresay head office can come up with someone.' He chuckled. 'Oh well, it will make a difference from fighting the environmental lobby; fortunately we've got everything covered on that aspect of it.'

She listened, aware that he had put his finger on the one thing that might give them an edge over their rivals. Mr McHale had not made a mistake when he sent John up here.

Almost to himself he went on, 'That must be it! A completely co-ordinated plan, dealing with every aspect of the set-up, from the time the fruit actually grows on the tree to the time the can leaves here in the ship. An anthropologist to advise on just how this foray into industrialism will affect the people, and how any effects can be minimised using the existing social set-up.' He chuckled suddenly. 'Thank heavens this is only the preliminary survey. We've got a few weeks to produce the goods. Well, I'll still have the Government to cope with, but the engineering team are coming on well, so Phil Redgrave tells me. I'll call a meeting of everyone tomorrow morning and discuss strategy.'

Tamsyn could have laughed her relief. 'You'll want me?'

'Yes. I'll send a car for you. We'll meet at the hotel—my sitting room is big enough for an informal meeting.'

It went well. The engineers were pleased with their progress, and the middle-aged Mr Robertson of the planning unit had not wasted his time. They approved John's angle, and made several suggestions to better their work, agreeing with him that it would all have to be looked at again in the light of the anthropologist's report.

Afterwards John kissed Tamsyn long and lingeringly, then put her away from him with determination.

'Work, my sweet! You have all of those reports to do, and I've got to get back to my siege of the Government.'

'Have you rung McHale?'

He chuckled, 'Yes. He must have wondered what the hell was going on, because I couldn't explain anything—you never know who might have been listening—but he's promised me my anthropologist. Isn't he a wonder? It arrives by plane tomorrow.'

'I'm sure that's the right way to tackle it,' Tamsyn said seriously. 'There was no doubt about Chapman's sincerity when he was talking about the islanders. He really loves them, John.'

'That will be our trump card. And that, my love, is perhaps where you can do even more important work than typing reports. Listen to him, ask him about the island, try to get his angle on things. If he offers to drive you around, accept, and keep pumping. Don't be obvious. He's clever, too clever for you; just be your normal interested self, and remember his answers, the tone of voice he speaks in. Women are good at that sort of thing, the personal angle.'

Perhaps Tamsyn's face revealed some of the acute distaste she felt for his assignment. John didn't know what he was asking of her—she was already far too aware of Grant Chapman!

Misinterpreting, he said swiftly, 'There's nothing underhand in it, darling. I know you don't like the man, but he is the key to this project. And he fancies you a tiny bit! He'd be less than a man if you didn't make some impression on him. Don't play on it, just accept it, and be your usual uncomplicated self with him. You may help far more than you realise, and you're in the ideal situation.'

Tamsyn felt wretchedly guilty. The temptation to tell John about that stolen kiss was strong—it seemed as though she could never feel clean again until he knew about it, but she forced herself to keep silent. The same reasons still applied. Perhaps she could assuage the guilt by doing just as John wanted.

Infusing some degree of lightness into her voice, she returned, 'OK, but he's a very attractive man, my love. Aren't you afraid I might get too interested in him?'

John laughed, catching her close in a big hug. 'I'll take the risk, sweet. Even if you do, I promise to wipe him completely from your mind once we're off this island.'

But it was not her mind Grant Chapman affected so strongly. It was a deeper, more primitive level that responded against the promptings of her brain to his intense masculinity. From the first she had known that he was a danger to her; now it seemed that John was forcing her deeper and deeper into a region of experience she had never even known existed.

'OK?' he said, but without doubting it for a moment. 'Oh, and don't mention the anthropologist. I don't want our Australian rivals getting any ideas. He'll be a member of the planning staff to anyone who asks.'

The reports kept Tamsyn busy all afternoon through the somnolent heat. At last, after making several foolish mistakes, she put them away and covered the typewriter, yawning. She felt drained of energy, but too restless to be able to relax, and decided to go for a brisk walk down to the beach to blow some cobwebs away.

The house was very quiet. Everyone would be either asleep or resting, waiting for the comparative coolness of evening before exerting themselves in any way. The stillness demanded soft movements from her. Feeling like a conspirator she donned sunhat and glasses and stole through the French doors, every nerve stretched almost to breaking point.

Away from the house it was less enervating, but still very hot. On an impulse Tamsyn left the path which Madame had told her led to the beach and wandered across the limp grass beneath the banana palms, gazing up at the huge hands of fruit all shades from vivid green to gold. Most were picked when they were green for export, but some were left to ripen for the house and the villagers. Perhaps she had walked in the green-gold gloom for ten minutes when she heard the soft thud of a horse's hooves on the grass, and turning saw Grant Chapman coming towards her mounted on a great grey gelding. Something odd happened to the pit of her stomach, but she ignored it, smiling faintly as he came up. He rode like a centaur, completely at one with the animal, a magnificent animal himself.

'Well met by sunlight, proud Titania,' he misquoted, halting beside her. 'Do you ride?'

'Yes.'

'I have a mare down in the stables who would probably suit you. Care to try her?'

Crushing back her instinctive refusal, she nodded.

'Yes, very much, thank you.'

'Good.' He bent, holding out an imperative hand. 'Come on up.'

Fortunately she was wearing slacks, but she had the feeling that it wouldn't have mattered if she had been attired in the most flowing of skirts. It was good to feel a horse beneath her again, but the close proximity of the man behind her made her desperately uneasy. She could feel the slow steady beat of his heart, the iron hard muscles of the arms against hers.

'Comfortable?' he asked mockingly as the grey turned back towards the house.

'It's a long time since I rode bareback, but yes, I'm comfortable.'

'How well do you ride?'

Without false modesty she answered, 'I used to be fairly good, but it's some time since I've done any.'

'Pony club?'

She laughed, remembering those days when life had been so free of complications. 'Yes.'

'They usually do a fairly good job of teaching the basics.'

A strange happiness flooded over her, a kind of reckless desire to ride peacefully like this for ever beneath banana palms on a tropical island. 'I learnt to ride on a cousin's sheep station,' she said idly. 'They put me up on a pony when I was two, and let me go. My mother was quite convinced that they were going to kill me, but I survived. No pony club strictness there! We rode around hills and through creeks, keeping on as best we could. When I was ten my uncle decided that we could help with the muster. I've never forgotten it, the noise and the dust and the heat, the incredible cleverness of the dogs and the equally incredible stupidity of the sheep.'

'You appear to be well equipped with relatives,' he commented.

'Hundreds of them. Mum and Dad both came from big

families. We always seemed to have someone staying.'

He shifted the reins to one hand, raised the other to brush away a lock of hair which had feathered across his mouth. 'And you the universal favourite, I suppose.'

Perhaps she had been, just as Sarah, bright tempestuous little Sarah, was now. Except that Tamsyn had always been considered a placid child. So why did her heart thump high in her throat, almost blocking it? She had been stupid to get up before him—asking for trouble! But it had seemed the only thing to do when confronted by that imperative hand.

'I don't know about that,' she murmured, trying hard to sound normal. 'I had a happy childhood.'

'And according to psychologists that gives you a head start on a normal adult life,' he said, the words a taunt. 'Lucky Tamsyn.' His free hand closed on her upper arm, then slid around her waist, pulling her back against the saddle. 'And now you're happily engaged to an up-and-coming young man, with nothing but happiness to look forward to.'

'Yes.' She said it defiantly, hating him for the physical effect he had on her, hating him even more for deliberately making use of it.

'You love him very much?'

Shamed colour flared on her cheekbones. She was glad he could not see her face. 'Very much,' she said firmly and clearly.

He laughed softly, releasing her. 'You must be a great help to him.'

Now what? she wondered angrily, before saying aloud, 'I hope so.'

'Oh, I'm sure you are. He's a lucky man.'

Through the trees she could see what must be the stables,

a low building, white beneath the shade of two huge trees, built so that it would catch any cool breath of wind.

He lifted her down, his fingers biting unnecessarily hard into her waist, then slung the reins over a post and took her in, his expression aloof and withdrawn once more.

The mare was a chestnut, mild of nature and strong, as she had need to be, for Tamsyn was no lightweight, in spite of her slimness. Her height and those unnecessarily wide shoulders saw to that. Brushing away the memory of how easily Grant Chapman had pulled her up on to his horse, she joined him as he made Sugar ready, and mounted before he had time to offer any help.

This time they rode up into the hills following a wide track which looked as if only horses or a Landrover ever used it. At first it was breathlessly hot, but when the banana palms gave way to real jungle growth it became cooler in the dimness. Tamsyn settled into the rhythm, watching as the mare's ears moved alertly. Grant Chapman could certainly pick horses, she told herself. Sugar was a delight to the eye, all grace and strength, while that grey in front was a magnificent creature. But then she could not imagine Grant ever being content with the second-rate. He would demand the best in anything he owned, from clothes to a wife. An odd little shiver feathered across her skin.

After about half an hour they emerged from the silent jungle on to a plateau where grass was short and crisp. Grant Chapman smiled mockingly at the surprise in her expression but said nothing. The grey responded to some unseen signal like the wind, showing a powerful pair of haunches. Tamsyn felt the impatience of her mount tingle through her and touched the sleek sides with her heels. Sugar took off after the two in front, obviously revelling in the comparative coolness of this hidden place.

The wind of their movement tore the smooth cap of Tamsyn's hair into tendrils of silver, brought a wild rose flush to her cheeks and a smile to her lips. For a little while all fears and worries left her in the sheer pleasure of a good mount beneath her and a place to ride it.

At last, reluctantly, she tightened the reins, pulling Sugar to a canter, then a walk, towards the clump of trees where Grant Chapman waited.

'That was marvellous!' she exclaimed, bending forward to pat Sugar's glossy neck, intimidated by the cold appraisal of his glance.

'You ride well. I'll give orders that Sugar is to be kept for you while you're here, but no riding by yourself.'

She looked up, surprised.

His smile was rather narrow. 'You don't know your way around. If I'm not here to go with you take Sulu, who lives in the compound by the house. Shout—he'll come running if he's not in the stable.'

Tamsyn nodded, aware of the sense of this remark. It would be highly inconvenient, to say the least, if she foolishly got lost and they had to mount a search party for her.

'Take a look at the view,' Grant said crisply.

It was magnificent. Beneath them lay the varied greens of the plantations in a verdant patchwork. Tamsyn picked out bananas, coconuts and pineapples, and a field where lilac and rose shimmered and blended.

'What's growing there?' she asked, pointing.

'Vanda orchids. One of the villagers went to Hawaii and saw them there. She found out as much as she could about growing them and came back with roots, and an immense amount of enthusiasm; the rest of the village were swayed by her into going into the business. They send them to

New Zealand and Australia and are doing very nicely.'

Tamsyn was impressed. 'I don't know why you worry about them. They seem to have enough business ability to survive.'

'Oh, they're astute enough, but not in a competitive atmosphere. I deal with their overseas interests, but with the higher standard of education more and more of them are moving into the administrative side. Family ties are very strong and the lure of the simple life always beckons, so it's a slow process.'

'It would be a pity if they lost the idyllic quality of their life.'

He slanted her a sharp glance. 'True. Unfortunately there have to be changes. One can only hope that the baby isn't thrown out with the bathwater.'

His comments reminded her of John's instructions to listen to everything that he said. Feeling like the cheapest spy she murmured, 'Just how do you envisage the island in, say, fifty years?'

Broad shoulders lifted in a shrug as he returned, 'I don't go in for wishful thinking, but for you, Tamsyn, anything. I'd like to see every child well versed in both Western education and his tribal lore, so that he can make an educated choice as to his future. There should be no tension between those who wish to follow a Western way of life and those who opt for the Polynesian; one should support the other. Perhaps both could be integrated to form a satisfactory life style.'

As he seemed to have finished, Tamsyn said tentatively, 'I suppose you'd like to see the island self-supporting.'

'Yes. Fortunately we've never suffered the worst forms of exploitation, so we do have a head start. These people are confident in their own worth; there's been very little cultural shock. Which is where this project which you're concerned with comes in. In effect we want a blueprint of the island's future.'

It was almost as though he had discovered her reasons for putting the question. Uneasily Tamsyn let her lashes droop to cover her too-candid eyes. Perhaps this was no news to John, but it certainly seemed to justify his decision to call in an anthropologist.

'No comment?' he asked mockingly.

'No—except that I hope you see your vision come true.'

'Ah, I'll be eighty-one if I do, and probably not in the least interested.'

So he was thirty-one. To say that she was surprised was perhaps a little exaggerated. Physically he seemed no more than that, but he had the air and authority of a man many years his senior and she had thought him older. No doubt it was because he had been in charge of his empire ever since he came of age, his parents having drowned when he was very young, and his grandfather dying soon after.

The mare whickered softly at the gelding, then moved slightly. Tamsyn looked far down the slopes to the gaudy green of the lagoon, with its purple patches where the water was shallow. A schooner was beating its way east, the westering sun touching the sails with gold. One of the island traders, no doubt, off to coral atolls and other high islands like this with a cargo of goods and laughing chattering Polynesians and their animals. An outrigger drifted lazily across the calm waters of the lagoon, while from the south a jet came in bearing a load of holidaymakers eager to escape winter in the sun and sand and sea of the tropics.

Tamsyn sighed.

'Homesick?'

'Oh, no!' she turned towards him, her emotions trans-

parent. 'It's so beautiful—and so peaceful. I was feeling
sorry that anything has to change.'

'You're too young for that,' he retorted caustically.
'Peace is for the elderly, my child, who've earned it.'

A sudden tension crackled between them. Her eyes
caught and held by the purposeful intensity of his, she felt
that unwarranted excitement tingling into life in her veins.
It had not been absent all through this ride, but she thought
it quiescent, only to discover that one look from him could
bring it flaming into life. He knew it, too. A small, set smile
curved his lips revealing a ruthlessness she was incapable of
facing. A pirate, she had thought him once. He looked all of
that now, determined to take what he wanted and not count
the cost. The excitement mounted as Tamsyn knew that he
wanted her.

For long moments she stared at him, then awkwardly
she slid from the mare, putting the animal's body between
her and a danger she only half understood. As she did so
John's diamond sparkled on her finger, a reminder which
brought shamed colour to her cheeks. Dear God, this must
not happen again! What ungodly temptation had persuaded
her into foolishly putting herself in a situation like this?
She would not be alone with him again.

One hand patted the gleaming neck beside her. Sounds
of movement told her that Grant too was dismounting, then
the mare moved away from her, as the reins were looped
over a convenient post. Sugar put down her head to crop
the grass. The grey stood still.

'Stay,' Grant said firmly, adding coolly, 'He won't stray.
Come on, I want to show you something.'

Feeling drained of will, Tamsyn allowed him to take her
hand, barely repressing a shudder at the firm touch of his

fingers against hers. What was the matter with her? Every instinct warned her of her stupidity, yet she did not protest as he guided her towards a rough track which led down into a thickly forested gully.

She was grateful for the support of his hand, for the track was rarely used, and great roots cut across it, making her stumble several times. Yet she was not normally clumsy.

No word passed between them. Indeed, he seemed to have withdrawn behind the mask of aloofness it appeared he could don at will. Tamsyn was relieved. That odd notion she had that he could see every emotion she felt must be false, born of her heightened awareness of him. No doubt he thought that he would give her something of the island to remember when she was back in wintry New Zealand. It had never seemed so far away now, her homeland, so safe and secure. A longing for her family wrenched at her heart. They were so—so sane, and sensible, they would provide her with the confidence she needed so badly at the moment. Without them she felt lost and alone, searching for some refuge from this situation she found herself in. At the moment she had no sanctuary; the old Tamsyn was being changed into someone new, someone who was venturing on uncharted seas, someone who was frightened and elated and ashamed all at once.

John, she thought feverishly, ducking a trailing fern frond. Desperately she tried to summon his beloved features in her mind's eye, but his face wavered then dimmed and became extinguished, leaving her cold and afraid.

'Here we are.'

Through Tamsyn's agonised thoughts the sound of water had been gradually percolating, at first a low hum in the distance, gradually increasing to a steady splash and surge. It came from a waterfall, a surge of water over rocks worn smooth by time.

Great ferns fringed it, their fronds glistening with spray like crystal filigree, while on the tall trees that backed them the native orchids bloomed, cream and pale lilac and gold, their delicate flowers emitting a sweet, slightly lemony scent. At the foot of the fall was a pool, wide and still and smooth in the sunlight, then another, smaller fall as the stream found its way down the slope towards the sea.

It was beautiful, the South Seas paradise the early explorers had written so feelingly about. Tamsyn freed her hand from Grant's clasp and went slowly towards the pool, her expression absorbed and wondering. A rock by the pool was exactly the right shape for a seat; it was warm and dry, and when Tamsyn sat on it she could trail her hand in water which was unexpectedly warm.

Grant's deep voice startled her. 'Can New Zealand show anything to compare?'

She smiled dreamily. 'Yes, but there would be no orchids and the water would be freezing cold. Oh—listen! What's that?'

The birdcall was soft but clear, the liquid notes like a series of violin notes.

'A *tikou* bird. You're lucky. They're elusive and not very common, living mostly on the peaks. The islanders say that if you hear one you'll get your heart's desire within a year.'

There was a note of derision in his voice which gave the comment a strangely personal sound. Tamsyn refused to look up, fighting the awareness of him which seemed to suffocate her. She would not allow herself to be beguiled into indiscretion by the unspoiled beauty of this place.

'Will you?' he asked after a moment.

'Will I what?'

'Get your heart's desire? When do you and Saunders plan to marry?'

'We haven't decided yet,' she almost whispered wretchedly, afraid of his probing.

He squatted down beside her, his shoulders level with hers, his expression cruelly taunting.

'If you were mine, I'd have you shackled close before you could get into trouble,' he stated.

Anger dilated her eyes, making them emeralds of fire.

'I'm not a slave to be shackled—nor am I likely to get into trouble,' she snapped, heavily sarcastic.

His mouth twisted. 'You already are, Tamsyn Forsythe. Deep in trouble.'

His closeness was intolerable. With nerves stretched to breaking point she sprang to her feet, but he rose with her, and when she would have run he caught her by the upper arms and held her, the steel bands of his fingers biting into the soft flesh as she twisted vainly.

'Don't—don't!' she whispered, afraid of the smouldering intensity of his gaze as it rested on her mouth.

'It's too late,' he said harshly, lips scarcely moving. 'And you know it.'

The kiss blotted out time and space for her, reducing her to a mindless thing at the mercy of emotions and feelings she had never known existed. As though intent on the ultimate conquest he threaded his fingers through the shining silk of her hair holding her head still, so that she could not pull her mouth away from the demanding pressure of his. After a few moments she no longer struggled, surrendering to his expert lovemaking with a readiness which was to appal her later. His mouth traced the fine contours of her face, closing her eyes with feather-light kisses, then swoop-

ing to her throat. Almost automatically Tamsyn grasped his
shoulders, then slid her hands around his neck, as she relaxed against him. It seemed right that he should pick her
up, right that after a few strides he should lay her on a bed
of soft grass and stretch himself beside her, but she did not
open her eyes, even when his hands touched her breast and
waist and thighs.

Lost in a golden haze of desire, every nerve vibrantly
alive even though his mouth and hands produced a dreamy
lassitude which sapped her will, she did not move as his
fingers undid the buttons of her blouse and began a more
intimate caress, smoothing the fine skin gently as his mouth
searched for and found the hollow between her breasts. A
flame of need so urgent that she felt it like a pain made her
moan softly and pull herself against him; dimly she was
aware that shame would come later, but for the moment she
was in thrall to a bondage far sweeter than any she had ever
dreamed of.

And then, even as his mouth covered hers in a kiss totally
unlike any she had ever experienced before, John's face
came to her mind, and with a half sob she twisted away,
clambering to her feet with desperate haste to stand pressed
against the trunk of one of the tall tree ferns, her trembling
hands pulling her blouse across her breasts to hide them,
her eyes shamed and pleading.

Grant got up slowly, looming above her like an avenging
pirate, his expression set in lines of contempt. Without
taking his smouldering eyes from hers he tucked his shirt
back into his trousers, then smiled, narrowly and without
amusement, as her trembling fingers fumbled with the buttons of her blouse.

'For heaven's sake!' he exclaimed crisply, and came up
to her and fastened the buttons himself.

Tamsyn bit her lip, a wave of colour flooding the clear skin. 'Grant—I——'

'Forget it. I got out of hand, and you had the sense to stop me.' He smiled again, but there was no warmth in the dark glance which raked her face.

'You're remarkably innocent for a girl contemplating marriage.'

Never had Tamsyn longed more fervently for longer hair! At least it would have hid the humiliation her too-expressive face revealed as she bowed her head. 'I—I'm sorry,' she stumbled.

'My dear girl, what on earth have you to be sorry for? I'm the one who's apologising!' His finger lifted her chin, forcing her to endure his cool scrutiny. 'Count it an experience. It should be a valuable one. Are you going to tell Saunders?'

The memory of her anguish, the difficult decision she had had to make before, made sudden tears sparkle in her eyes.

Grant said something under his breath and wiped them away, saying roughly, 'For heaven's sake, Tamsyn! Do you want me to kiss you better, because that's what you're inviting! Shall I tell him?'

'No!' She shivered. 'No, I—I'll tell him. And—I think perhaps I'd better go back to the hotel.'

'I can see no reason for that.' He smiled slightly at her bewilderment. 'Oh, I'll grant that I find you desirable, but contrary to what you may have heard, I don't have an affair with every beautiful woman who happens to attract me. And Grand'mère enjoys your company.'

But she shook her head, aware that in his oddly kind mood he was far too much of a threat to her peace of mind. If only it was just her peace that he threatened! Miserably she faced the fact that he had the power to overthrow the whole structure of her hitherto peaceful life, leaving nothing but ruin in his path.

'Talk it over with Saunders,' he advised calmly. 'He seems a sensible chap. I doubt if he'll hold one small step from the straight and narrow path of rectitude against you. Or me.'

CHAPTER FOUR

On the way back he talked about the project, discussing with her his hopes and plans for it. Sick at heart, Tamsyn forced herself to respond, knowing that John would want to know everything he had said.

She felt torn in two, guilty and confused and weary with a bone-deep tiredness which did not have its roots in any physical cause. It seemed that Grant was trying to restore her confidence in herself with his quiet conversation, and this bewildered her anew. Perhaps she had mistaken that flash of contempt in his eyes when he had buttoned her blouse for her. She did not know him very well, after all, and he could not have been more understanding since then. Brushing aside the uneasy feeling that he revealed only as much of himself as he wanted she found herself reassured by his matter-of-fact behaviour, but knew that she could have no relief from the shame that she was sure must be apparent in her very face, until she had told John. It had been easy enough to convince herself that he should not hear of one kiss, but those embraces by the waterfall had not been in the same category!

She had suffered an all-out onslaught on her emotions as well as her body, and she had responded only too willingly, forgetting completely the vows she had exchanged—forgetting John's existence as if he had never put his ring on her finger.

At least, she thought drearily, she had had the self-control not to let the incident proceed to its inevitable conclusion when her every instinct had been to give in to his virile needs—just as if she was an untaught adolescent completely at the mercy of her wayward body. Thank God for that!

There could be no easing of her mind until the next day, because John was not coming to the plantation until after he had met the anthropologist on the morning's plane.

The evening began wretchedly. As a starter Liz Holland was there again, strikingly beautiful in lilac silk. She looked like one of the orchids which had given the area around the waterfall its fairy-tale beauty, and there was no doubt that she was in love with Grant Chapman. Her almond eyes lingered on his face when he spoke, her voice had a more intimate note in its husky tones when she addressed him, and she constantly referred to occasions they had shared, effectively cutting Tamsyn out of much of the conversation.

There were others there too, two married couples, and the same elderly Captain Marsh who had escorted Madame the first night they had met. There was also a Frenchman, Monsieur de la Tour, who was a relation of Madame's and called by Grant 'mon oncle.'

It was he who sat beside Tamsyn at dinner and paid grave court to her, his dark eyes gravely admiring as they rested on her face. It was pleasant to be admired in a way which presented no threat; Tamsyn relaxed, and several times that rich laughter of hers was heard, subdued but still with the irrepressible note of amusement which made it so attractive.

After dinner he came to sit beside her, saying cheerfully, 'Allow me to make up in some small part for the absence of you betrothed, mademoiselle. He is busy tonight?'

Tamsyn nodded, her expression clouding a little. 'Yes, I'm afraid so.'

'Ah, these businessmen!' He cast a deprecating glance at Grant. 'Never is the business forgotten, not even when they play.'

Rather daringly Tamsyn asked, 'Are you not in business, monsieur?'

'No, not at all. I am a farmer from Nouvelle Cal-edonie—New Caledonia, you call it. There we have extensive plains with good grass, a little like the plateaux here, but much, much more of them, and we grow cattle. Also coffee, for export. Not the best coffee, but still very good.' His eyes twinkled appreciatively as she smiled.

Tamsyn found herself liking him very much. He was quietly amusing, and made it obvious that he gained pleasure from her company without embarrassing her with compliments as a younger man might have done. Nice, without being dull, a considerable contrast to his English relative!

Somehow she learned that he was a widower with a son at school in France, that he had arrived in the afternoon to stay for a few days with his cousin, whom he called Solange. 'Then I go on to Fiji, and from there to France after a short stay in the United States looking at cattle.'

Tamsyn was interested, as befitted the daughter of a cattle breeder, 'Special ones, monsieur?'

'Yes. I hope to import some from the Gulf coast where they have bred them to resist heat. I believe that they are also being tested in the northern parts of New Zealand, where the climate is sub-tropical.'

'Yes, I've heard of them, but I'm afraid I don't know much about them. My father breeds dairy cattle—Jerseys.'

'Ah, yes, I have been to Jersey Island. It is an enchanting place, and the cattle impressed me immensely—graceful as deer. Your father has visited it, perhaps? It is a place of pilgrimage for breeders.'

She laughed, shaking her head. The light caught in the spun silver of her hair, turning it into an aureole of molten moonlight about her head. 'When he retires in a few years' time, he and Mum are going on a world tour, and Jersey Island is on the agenda.'

'It will be the first time they have travelled?'

'Except for a couple of holidays in Australia.'

'And you also?' he asked. 'Is this your first time out of your beautiful homeland?'

Tamsyn nodded. 'Yes.'

'Ah, to be young and eager again. Fala'isi is beautiful, is it not?'

'Far more lovely than I'd hoped for. One hears so much about the South Sea Islands that I was afraid the reality might be disappointing.'

He smiled, his dark eyes almost dreamy as they rested on her face. 'I'm glad it has not proved to be so. Be careful, mademoiselle, for the lure of the tropics is like an insidious disease creeping unfelt through the veins until one succumbs. Grant's grandfather fell victim to it, and could not leave, and although in some ways it would make life easier for Grant to move to Australia or even Europe, he prefers to run his empire from here.'

Involuntarily Tamsyn's glance had flown to the master of the house, tall and very masculine as he bent to listen to his grandmother.

The man beside her said quietly, 'One lives at a slower

but richer pace in the islands. The passions run higher here; one either succumbs or develops immense self-control to overcome them. Things have a habit of looking so different where frangipani scents the air and the trade winds blow.'

Could he be warning her? Or was it merely that the memory of what it was like being held in those strong arms had the power to colour her every thought, making her absurdly sensitive to hitherto unheard nuances in a voice? Tamsyn looked down at the engagement ring as if to draw strength from the promise it represented, but it only served to make her feel hollow at the thought of what she had to tell John. His reaction fretted at the back of her mind. He had every right to be angry and disappointed, but surely he would not completely lose trust in her. I must leave here, she thought desperately, unaware that the green mystery of her eyes had become darkened with pain and frustration.

'It appears that we are to have some music,' the man beside her said after a long moment. 'Miss Holland loves to dance.'

Especially with Grant Chapman, Tamsyn thought wearily, wishing herself back in the comfortable familiarity of her bedroom on the farm. A sudden longing for her mother almost brought tears to her eyes. Vivienne Forsythe with her calm good sense and warmly loving nature which nothing ever shocked would know exactly how her daughter should behave to get herself out of the trap which seemed to have been sprung around her. But Vivienne was hundreds of miles away over the rolling waters of the Pacific, and Tamsyn must battle along on her own, unable to find sanctuary even in the company of the man who loved her.

At least Monsieur de la Tour was an understanding partner. And a good one. But after that they changed, and

Tamsyn found herself where she had vowed never to be again, back in Grant Chapman's arms. Tension prickled along her skin, but she forced herself to relax, aware that he would have no compunction about commenting on her lack of enthusiasm.

Instead he asked somewhat aloofly, 'Has my French uncle been entertaining you sufficiently?'

'Yes. He's nice.'

'Oh, very. Full of subtle Gallic charm, and with a Frenchman's eye for beauty, especially blonde beauty.'

Tamsyn flushed at the derisive note in his voice, but said nothing, her eyes fixed firmly on her ring as it glittered against the white material of his jacket. Like an automaton she followed his lead while the dark enchantment of his personality enveloped her. It was so unfair! She wanted nothing of him—nothing, and yet without even trying he possessed some sort of magnetism which pulled her, resist as much as she would, further and further into a bondage she both dreaded and feared.

The evening wore on. Madame played bridge with her contemporaries, not too seriously, there was wine and more dancing, some conversation, and then, at last, it was time for the guests to go. When Grant's car had purred off down the drive Tamsyn turned to her hostess and said her goodnights, grateful that it was over.

She showered in barely warm water, pulled on a short cotton nightgown and wrap and brushed her hair, willing herself to relax enough for sleep. Never had a bed seemed more inviting, and never had sleep been so far away! Like a restless ghost she prowled around her room, her eyes wide and tragic. If only John were here, so that she could rid herself of this burden of guilt, be reassured by his beloved presence! The house seemed an alien thing, holding back as it watched her, passively rejecting one who had no right to be here.

What is the matter with me, she almost cried aloud, pushing her hands through her hair in an unconscious imitation of John's gesture. Was she so frail that her love could not stand up to temptation, even though it was a kind she had never faced before, had never even known to exist? That a woman could love one man and desire another with every fibre of her being sickened her; nothing in her life had prepared her for such a revelation of her own weakness, yet it was something which must be faced and overcome.

Like Lucifer, Grant Chapman had come into her life; a dark angel of foreboding who appealed to the sensual side of her nature. She shivered as she remembered those moments when she had surrendered to his mastery of her, wanting only to lose herself in complete union with him. Such abandon was foreign to her and the memory of it made her feel unclean.

And yet, she thought, trying hard for objectivity, if she was fair she must admit that his personality too had a profound impact on her. She had never before met a man who combined arrogance with the kind of charm which rightfully belonged to the Continent, a charm which he must know he possessed though he had not used it deliberately as far as she knew. He had not set out to dazzle her into an unwilling attraction; reluctantly she admitted that whatever reaction he kindled in her was the result of her own weakness, one which he took advantage of.

And that was the worst thing she knew of him. He should not kiss her when he knew that she was an unwilling captive; it revealed an opportunism in him that hurt for some strange reason. Apart from that, he was a man you could respect for his intelligence and his character, even if he did live like a lord in this house filled with treasures, surrounded by a horde of servants who all seemed to admire him immensely. Certainly there was none of the stiffness and formality that Tamsyn had vaguely assumed would be the hallmark of a society where servants were taken for granted. The women who worked here obviously adored him, while the men were respectful but not in the least intimidated.

It was impossible to separate the man from his wealth or the power he yielded both on the island and 'out over', as Tamsyn had heard one of the girls refer to the world outside Fala'isi. The wealth and the power were as integral a part of Grant Chapman as his darkly handsome features and his lithe stride.

Yet, Tamsyn thought, wretchedly aware that she was far too interested in Grant Chapman, if he were stripped of every outward thing that seemed so much a part of him he would still be a man to respect for his strength came from within, from his character.

And if this attraction she felt was just a thing of the senses then his character should mean nothing to her.

The implications of this drove her to further restless pacing. She could not be falling in love with him! To love one man and want another could be possible. It was quite impossible to love two men at the same time, and she loved John, needed him as she had never needed him before, thought of him with yearning. He *must* agree that she leave this place: if she no longer trusted herself how could he feel any trust for her? Certainly not enough to leave her here in a situation which, as she was beginning to understand, held danger for her, danger made greater by the fact that she could discern exactly where it lay.

The last remembrance she had of the night was when, exhausted and more miserable than she had ever been before, she almost collapsed on to the side of the bed. When she woke she was in the bed. Amazing what the unconscious could do, she thought bleakly, observing her robe neatly slung over the back of a chair.

With the morning things did not seem quite as despairing as they had in the long watches of the night, but as she walked through the house she was more determined than ever to leave. She could make the anthropologist her excuse—say that it was inconvenient to be here when there was extra work. Madame might be disappointed, but Tamsyn hardened her heart; after all, once this survey was done they would never meet again.

Usually Tamsyn was the only person at the breakfast table, but today, of course, Grant had to be there, devilishly confident as she came towards the shady arbour on the terrace where the table had been set.

He rose, unsmiling, and put her in a chair. Tamsyn murmured 'Good morning' in a stifled voice, refusing to meet his eyes in case she should see derision in the grey depths.

The smell of coffee was refreshing, teasing her nostrils. When she poured herself a cup Grant pushed his cup across so that she was forced to give him another. He took it black, with no sugar, as though treating a hangover she thought irrelevantly, sliding her spoon into the pale gold flesh of a grapefruit.

'Did you sleep well?'

The question surprised her. 'Yes, thank you,' she returned in a cool little voice.

'Good.'

A dreadful suspicion assailed her. With spoon poised she

looked up, met the mocking laughter of his glance and could not prevent the blush which revealed her unsureness.

'Next time, put the light out,' he observed drily. 'I couldn't believe my eyes when I got home at three and saw it on, Did you take something to make you sleep? You didn't stir when I put you to bed.'

She bit her lip, then released it. 'I sleep like the dead once I get off. Thank you.'

'Nicely spoken,' he mocked. 'Even if you don't mean it. I could have got one of the maids out of bed, but it seemed a little unfair.'

'It would have been.'

Apparently tiring of teasing her, he enquired blandly, 'And what do you intend to do this morning?'

'Work,' she stated with no attempt at elaboration.

'When do you expect to see Saunders again?'

'Oh, some time today,' she answered, purposefully vague.

He gave her a narrow smile but said nothing more, leaving her prey to some devastating emotion which had leapt into full-blown life when he told her that he had not arrived home until three. It could not be jealousy, but she pushed the thought of him making love to Liz Holland to the furthest recesses of her mind and applied herself to the grapefruit with a grim determination which deserved a more worthy cause.

The coffee eased the tight knot of tension within her, although she could not eat any more than the fruit and a crisp Continental roll. The air was still cool, but the sun was bounding higher into the sky, drawing up the dew in a fine gossamer mist which rapidly faded into nothingness in the warm air. A bird sang a few notes, then was gone, an arrow of blue into the scarlet blossoms of a poinciana tree, no doubt to gorge on the nectar. Clumps of palms lifted feathery arms to the sky, their ribbed trunks straight and slender, festooned with great clusters of gold berries which glittered in the sun. Coffee cup in hand, Tamsyn rose and walked across the terrace to stand beside a tubbed gardenia.

Rude or not, she had to get away from Grant, even if only for a few moments. He had too potent an effect on her! The gardenia blossoms were creamy white, their scent strong, more of night and its erotic enchantment than the cool sanity of day. Slowly, as if impelled, Tamsyn turned back to the table and to the man who sat there; for the first time she admitted to herself that distance might not lessen the effect he had on her, that in all the wide world there might be no sanctuary from whatever it was that he had wakened into life within her.

The realisation horrified her but, paradoxically, strengthened her determination to leave the plantation and this too close intimacy, where he could put her into her bed without her realising it. John must not insist that she stay, on the offchance that she could learn something of use to him. Grant was too clever to give anything away unless for a reason.

John came mid-morning, smiling, obviously much more calm than he had been when last they saw each other, and whisked her off to the hotel in a car he had hired for the rest of his stay on the island.

Tamsyn hated to spoil the mood of gaiety he was wrapped in, but after a few false starts managed to gain his attention.

'Something important to tell me?' he asked eagerly. 'Go on, love.'

Baldly, without any details, she told him exactly what

had transpired beside the waterfall, her tension clear in each sparse word.

John's hands clenched on the wheel. After a few seconds he swung the car on to the grass verge beneath a great pandanus palm and listened, staring straight ahead as her cool, dull voice unfolded the sordid little story. Of her own emotions she said nothing, even yet refusing to face the fact that Grant Chapman had an effect on her which could not be explained.

When her voice faltered to a stop he turned, pulling her swiftly into his arms. 'It's OK,' he murmured softly. 'Poor kid, you've had a rugged time, and it's all my fault. Don't cry, love; I don't blame you in the least. I knew what sort of man he was. I should have warned you.'

'John——'

He hugged her tightly. 'It's just as well you aren't the passionate type, sweetie, or you could have found yourself in real trouble.'

This was terrible! Somehow he had managed to see everything quite wrong. She touched his cheek, saying urgently, 'But darling, I——'

'Hush, no more worrying about it. I forbid you to! At least you know now the sort of guy he is, so you can avoid any situations like that again. It must have given you quite a shock.'

'Please!' she exclaimed desperately, realising that she must tell him everything.

He stopped any confession with a kiss, light but long enough to reveal that he had no intention of allowing her to pursue the subject. 'No, you listen to me. I suppose he got carried away—you're lovely enough to make any man feel lightheaded; did he apologise?'

'I—yes, he did,' she admitted, wondering wretchedly what to say next.

'Fair enough. He won't try it again, I'm sure.' He hugged her again, smiling in a forced way which wrung her heart. 'Darling, don't *worry* about it. OK, so you've had a shock —and that's my fault, because I know his reputation, and I should have warned you. Not that I thought he'd try anything with you. No, don't say anything. I won't pretend not to be jealous—I am, but being a man myself I can see exactly why Chapman behaved as he did, and quite frankly, Tamsyn, if you want me to punch his nose, I'm not going to!'

'I don't,' she whispered forlornly, wondering why she was not more comforted by his briskly sensible way of looking at the incident which had cost her so much heartburn and anguish. It was almost as though he was refusing to see any deeper implications in the matter because he was so determined to win this contract that he would sacrifice anything, even his fiancée's peace of mind, for it.

That was a horrible, disloyal thought: ruthlessly she pushed it to the back of her mind.

'Then that's OK,' John murmured, releasing her. 'Just make sure not to be so alone with him again—although I'm certain that as you have shown him that you are not the sort of girl who plays around he'll not try anything else. He wouldn't do anything against that stiff English code of honour.'

Tamsyn ran her fingers through her tousled hair, biting her lip. 'I thought—I'd rather go back to the hotel,' she said baldly.

His reaction was abrupt and hurtful. 'No way, Tamsyn. You may not realise it, but the conversations you've reported have been of considerable help.' He switched the engine on, frowning slightly. 'Actually, love, I'll get you to tape anything new from now on, so that the anthropologist can hear exactly what you have to say. You'll like her, by the way. She's middle-aged and vague, but only when it concerns anything not connected with her field. McHale says she's extremely good. A string of letters after her name, and she's written several books which probably no one but other anthropologists have read.'

As they drove into town he continued speaking lightly and easily, as though she had never told him of the moments she had spent in Grant Chapman's arms. Tamsyn forced herself to follow his lead, but the hollow bubble of despair within her grew. Between them he and Grant were forcing her on to a path she could only find despicable. Every feeling rebelled against further contact with Grant, every instinct of self-preservation warned her that she was in grave danger from him, yet John would not admit it, would not allow her to do the only thing possible and get as far away from the danger as she could. Perhaps because to do so would be admitting that Grant was a threat to their happiness. Or perhaps because he was prepared to go to any lengths to get this contract for McHale's.

The insidious treachery of the thought came unbidden again, like a thief in the night, and this time would not be banished. With an effort Tamsyn stilled the writhing of her hands, realising that she could not ignore this suspicion which had pushed its way through the layers of her consciousness. If she refused to face it it could poison her relationship with John, and already that was in jeopardy because of her wanton response to Grant's calculated passion. And what seemed to be the even greater calculation of John's reaction to that. If only he had been angry with her, accused her of duplicity! Anything would have been more reassuring than his calm levelheadedness. Surely it was unnatural?

The thoughts twisted and turned like snakes through her mind, exhausting her into a silence which passed unnoticed in John's light conversation. When they arrived at the hotel it was for a conference: Tamsyn took notes, glad of the concentration needed. At least she could not think while scribbling shorthand! It went on all day, through the hot humid hours after lunch, each member of the team putting forward suggestions, all of them discussing each one at length before listening respectfully to the slim, elegantly grey-haired woman who was Margot Henderson, the anthropologist. In spite of that impressive string of letters after her name she was extremely practical, making comments which were blunt and very much to the point.

At last it was over. Tamsyn made a wry grimace as she looked at the pile of stuff she had to cope with, because there were tapes to deal with as well as paper.

'A good several days' work,' Margot Henderson said casually. 'Your boss is an efficient man, Miss Forsythe, I see he expects the same efficiency from his secretary.'

John came back into the room, smiling so broadly that it would not have surprised Tamsyn to see him rubbing his hands. 'They've all gone,' he announced unnecessarily. 'Let's have a drink to celebrate. I think we're getting things into some sort of order.' He smiled at the anthropologist, his charm so blatant that Tamsyn almost blinked. 'You were a great help, Mrs Henderson.'

'It's a pleasure to work for a company responsible enough to employ someone like me,' the older woman returned promptly. 'Conservation is the "in" thing now, of course, but it's rare to find a firm paying more than lip service to it.

Even rarer to find one prepared to put its money where its mouth is.'

John poured vodka and lime, smiling broadly. 'My brainwave, and a good one, I think.' He began to talk of the necessity for industry to take a lead instead of following trends, expanding on the theme for some minutes. He sounded as though he was addressing a meeting.

Tamsyn sipped her drink, watching him from beneath half-closed lids, her lashes effectively veiling her thoughts. Lassitude seeped through her, tying her to the chair, keeping her silent as John talked eagerly on. She felt unable to fight anything any more, as though a fatalism she had never known she possessed had taken over. There was nothing she could do about anything, it seemed, except allow the tide of events to carry her wherever it went.

It did not surprise her that John sent her back alone in the car. He was due at the house of a government official for dinner, and his farewell was almost perfunctory. When she clung to him, hoping for reassurance, he put here away after a moment, saying teasingly, 'Another time, sweetie.'

There was mail for her too. A letter from her mother and one from Sarah. Waiting until she was back at the plantation to read them Tamsyn found that home seemed very far away compared to the scent of the white ginger in her nostrils, the brilliance of the croton leaves, the warm caress of the soft air.

Madame found her down by a clear pool staring down into water starred by pink and gold waterlilies.

'Ah, you choose a quiet place to read your letters,' she remarked. 'All is well?'

Tamsyn smiled into the older woman's shrewd eyes. 'Yes, my little sister is learning to play hockey and finds it very exciting. Also my sister-in-law thinks she's pregnant, so everyone is excited about that.'

'Indeed, it is news of great importance, then. How long have they been waiting for this baby?'

Tamsyn obeyed her gesture and sank down on a stone bench in the shade of a tree of heaven. Before them the sun gleamed in great shafts through the leaves of the palms, gilding the grass. It was quiet and very peaceful.

'Rod and Lesley have been married for three years.'

'So long?' Madame looked faintly scandalised. 'Ah, but I forget the modern way of life. It is not now common practice to begin one's family immediately.'

'I don't think Lesley would have minded,' Tamsyn replied. 'They're living in the worker's cottage on the farm, so she would have had Mum to help her.'

'She would not object?'

'No.' Tamsyn breathed a small sigh. 'Lesley has no family of her own, and she and my mother are like mother and daughter.'

'You are fond of her also?'

'It would be impossible not to be. She's so gay and gallant, a tiny little thing with brown curls and laughing brown eyes.'

'Your brother is blond, like you?' Madame prompted.

'Honey-coloured hair, but darker-skinned. The same green cat's eyes. He's tall and quiet—we say that he and Dad must communicate by gestures, because neither of them say much. They say that we women talk so much that they can't get a word in edgeways.'

Madame chuckled. 'A typical masculine statement! Your good mama must be excited over the prospect of a grandchild.'

'Very. So is my little Sarah. She tells me that she will be the first aunt in her classroom.'

There was a short silence, then Madame said almost to herself, 'Grant's mother hoped for many children, but alas, it was not to be. He was a large baby, so after him there could be no more. Then she and my Gregory went sailing in the lagoon and a squall came up. They both drowned, and I was left with a five-year-old to bring up.' She stirred, looked up into the sympathetic face of the girl beside her and went on briskly, 'An old tragedy, *ma petite*. I had hoped that Grant would marry early, as Gregory did, but he has not so far met the woman he can fall in love with, so I must wait for my great-grandchildren.'

A peculiar sensation exploded in Tamsyn's bones. Rushing into speech, she said, 'You must have been very young when you had your—Grant's father, Madame.'

'Seventeen only. And I thank you for the compliment, my child. Women age quickly in the tropics, but English-women faster than we of darker skin and hair, I think, and Fala'isi is kinder than most. There is no malaria or yellow fever and the climate does not reach the extremes of places closer to the Equator.'

'It's like paradise,' Tamsyn murmured softly, her glance wistful as she gazed around at the trees and the pool, felt the warmth of the breeze on her bare arms.

'The only paradise is a pair of loving arms,' Madame said drily, then laughed. 'Ah, now my secret is out! Grant calls me his practical romantic, and I fear he is correct. We French have been forced down the centuries to allow the practical side of our nature to become predominant, but the desire for romance is always there. Grant has it also, otherwise he would have married some eminently suitable woman long before this. Instead he looks for one to love, and spends his time with other, less demanding woman.'

A faint flush warmed Tamsyn's cheeks. Was Madame warning her?

'You are surprised that I know of his *affaires*?' The older woman gave a very Gallic shrug. 'What would you? He is a virile man, and rich, and there are always women willing to accept less than a wedding ring. And he is a man who stirs women's hearts to longing, just as his grandfather was, as Gregory was. The woman Grant marries will have to trust him absolutely, for she will not be able to trust her own sex with him.'

Tamsyn could not help her sudden delighted chuckle. 'You're a cynic, Madame.'

'A realist, rather.' But Madame seemed well pleased with the effect of her comments. 'You have an unusual beauty, Tamsyn. Not at all conventional, with your wide shoulders and long, long legs and that short straight hair, but one cannot forget you. At first I thought it was the colouring, so rare in this day of well-tanned women, but I do not think so now. Although your features are not startling they are irradiated by those eyes and your laughter.' She chuckled at the embarrassment on the girl's face, and leaned forward to touch her hand for a moment. 'Be tranquil, *ma petite*. I do not discuss you with anyone, but an old woman has much time to sit and think.'

'An old woman?' Tamsyn teased. 'You're ageless, Madame.'

'Like the Sphinx? I think not. Come, let us go back to the house. Shortly we shall have more visitors, a party of Grant's friends from the United States. I must note down a few things to remember. My memory, alas, is no longer as efficient as it should be. While they are here we shall have a big party. Remind me to ask that handsome fiancé of yours.'

A party in such beautiful surroundings should be something to remember for the rest of one's life, Tamsyn thought as they walked side by side towards the white luxury of the house. At least John would be there.

CHAPTER FIVE

INDOORS it was cool and shady, quiet except for the sound of golden laughter in the distance. One of the maids enjoying life, as they always seemed to.

'Ah, there you are,' Madame said to her grandson as he came through the door of his office. 'You are busy?'

'I've just finished.' Grey eyes met green in an ironic glance. 'You look weary, Miss Forsythe.'

'Like you, I've had a busy day.'

'And letters from home,' Madame put in. 'She is a little *triste*, I think, a little homesick.'

Grant looked at the blue airmail envelopes in Tamsyn's hand. 'I wondered what had taken the sparkle from that smile,' he murmured, a note of mockery in the deep tones. 'Well, we can't have you moping. I'm going down to the village to see someone. Would you like to come?'

In the little silence caused by Tamsyn's hesitation Madame urged, 'Yes, go with him, Tamsyn. It is pleasant down there, and perhaps a novel experience will help you forget all those weary miles between your little sister and you.'

Without making herself awkward and discourteous Tamsyn could not refuse, but the glance she darted at her host was mutinous and more than a little angry.

He smiled. 'You'd better put on a longer dress. The Polynesians object to the sight of women's knees, although they're remarkably casual about clothing for the upper body—in the villages, at least.'

'Yes, you will have to sit on mats,' Madame agreed. 'Ua'ili refuses to allow any western innovations into his village except for sewing machines.'

Tamsyn retired in good order, put on a long flounced skirt of gold cotton patterned with beige flowers and a blouse of the same gold, sleeveless but with a high shirt collar. In spite of his remark about the women's practice of going naked above the waist when at home she was not going to reveal any more than she had to! Slipping her feet into leather thongs, she determined wearily not to allow herself to be lured into any false position. Madame had made it impossible for her to refuse to be alone with him, but she had no intention of turning her back to the danger he represented.

Unfortunately it seemed that everything conspired against her, because when she reappeared Grant told her that he intended to walk the half mile or so to the village, and it seemed churlish to protest that she would rather get there more quickly in a car.

As they went through the perfumed beauty of the garden that sense of fatalism came stealing back over her, and with it an acceptance of the situation. Just exactly what her emotions towards the man beside her were she did not know, but there was no denying that when she was with him excitement bubbled through her veins, and her every sense seemed sharpened, so that her eyes saw more beauty, her ears were keener, and life tasted good in her mouth.

'You've not been to a native village, I presume,' he said after a few moments.

'No. I've been on *maraes* in New Zealand, though.'

'You'll have a rough idea of how to behave, then, although these people have not adopted any part of the Western way of life, and the conventions are strict. You must remove your shoes before entering the *fale*, and sit down as soon as you're there in front of a post. Sit cross-legged—stretching your legs out is extremely rude. If you get cramp, you can tuck your legs beside you, but cover them with a mat, and whatever you do, don't point your toes at anyone. It's a deadly insult.'

Tamsyn looked up, wondering just how he managed to remain comfortable in that position. With a mocking smile he said softly, 'I'm used to it. I spent a lot of my time down here when I was a scruffy kid.'

'Were you scruffy?' she asked idly.

'All boys are scruffy, unless there's something wrong with them. Why should I be any different?'

'No reason,' she said, then hurriedly turning the conversation away from this personal note, 'Is there anything else I should know?'

He sounded amused at the transparent manoeuvre, but returned, 'They'll offer us food, probably fruit and drinking nuts. You must eat and drink. After that I'll talk to Ua'ili; his wife will probably take you to the women's part of the house and show you her treasures. She'll offer them all to you—accept one.'

'Oh no!' Tamsyn protested.

'Oh, yes. Don't worry, they'll be mostly pretty shells, fans—that sort of thing. If you don't take one she'll think you consider them a poor selection. You'll have an opportunity later of returning a gift.' He reached out and touched her hair, tugging a strand. 'She'll probably want to stroke this. All of the village knows that I have a *papalagi* at my house with hair like the moonpath on the lagoon. Don't be surprised if you're surrounded by small children as soon as you leave me. And don't worry about behaving badly. They know you aren't used to their customs.'

The touch of his hand confused her, but it acted as a very salutary reminder of the vow she had made not to allow him any more intimacies. On the pretext of removing a pebble from her sandal she bent, and when she straightened took care to remain a pace away from him.

The path was a broad one winding beside the little stream which threaded through the wild garden at the plantation. Instead of the sickly green light of the banana palms they walked in the cool dimness of a remnant of the native vegetation, a mini-jungle where ferns drooped over the limpid waters and the wild hibiscuses caught the sun in shimmering splendour. It ended on a grassy knoll above the village where thirty or so *fales* sheltered in a tiny valley. Coconut palms bent gracefully over the beach, shading canoes and small children, the thatched roofs drowsed quietly under spreading trees, each on a neat platform of dazzling white crushed coral.

'That's where we're going,' Grant said softly, nodding at a slightly larger home, set a little higher than the rest. 'No one must overlook the chief.'

'What are the smaller *fales*?' Tamsyn asked, enchanted by the doll's house tidiness of the scene.

'The cooking *fales*. It's almost sundown, so most of the women will be waiting for the food to cook in the *umu*, the earth oven.'

'Oh, like a *hangi* at home.' Tamsyn smiled reminiscently.

'Exactly. The men do all of the hard work, but the women prepare and serve the meal. Do you like food cooked in an earth oven?'

'Love it. When my brother Rod became engaged to Lesley we had one for them. Friends of ours put it down, and it was superb.'

He nodded, 'Perhaps you'll have a chance to compare the two. Ah, we've been seen.'

A child called out a greeting, then turned and scuttled off towards the chief's *fale*, yelling something as he went. With a little sigh Tamsyn followed Grant down the slope towards the village, to be greeted with immense dignity by the old, silver-haired chief and his portly wife.

It happened just as he had predicted. Before Tamsyn's muscles had had time to cramp in the sitting position, she had partaken of slices of mango and the cool sweet milk of the coconut and was escorted by Lisialu towards the cooking *fale*, Grant having mentioned that she came from New Zealand and was interested in the differing ways of cooking.

Women were much the same the world over, she thought, as her hostess revealed in accented English recipes for some of the food that was cooked. And children too, smiling at one three-year-old in his big sister's arms, who had touched her hair with tentative fingers. Her smile was the signal for every other child to hold out a hand and beg to be allowed to stroke her tresses.

'No—no——' Lisialu protested, but it was easy to see from her half-hearted gesture that children were spoiled here, and when she saw that Tamsyn did not mind she stood with hands on her ample hips and organised the children into a queue.

One of the older girls murmured something and on being reprimanded for not speaking English said shyly, 'It is like Rongo, the moon girl, when she smiles from the skies.'

Tamsyn was enchanted with the compliment, thinking

wistfully that it had been a long time since she had heard one so sincere. Then Lisialu shooed everyone away and took her guest down to the beach; a child came running with a shell, fan-shaped and tiny, pale tangerine over pearl, handing it to Tamsyn with a gamin grin before tearing down to the water and plunging in with several others.

'They are cheeky,' the big woman beside her said fondly. 'That one is my son's son. He goes to the school and can read and write better than all of the others in his class. He says that he is going to become a doctor, but I think he will end up as chief, like his grandfather.' She chuckled, 'One of my daughters is in New Zealand. She writes that it is cold and very big, but that the people are friendly. She is training to be a teacher. My sons say that she should marry, but my husband told her, "Learn as much as you can for the honour of your family and your island." Grant helps us to keep her there,' she ended matter-of-factly.

Tamsyn nodded. 'Will she come back here when she finishes her training?'

'Oh yes, that is understood. We have nurses and teachers there training, and one boy from the other side of the island is almost a doctor. Grant's grandfather started the scheme, oh, forty years ago. Now the government helps, but Grant does much. He is an islander also, like us.'

As they talked she had been steering them back towards the *fale*. Grant and the white-haired old chief had been joined by several other men, all middle-aged or older. It came as no surprise to hear him speak in the language of the islanders, the soft, mellow syllables rolling easily off his tongue.

Lisialu kept her precious things in a wooden chest in one corner; she displayed them proudly, smiling at Tamsyn enthused over a necklace of tiny green shells and pressed it into her hands.

'Take it, to remember us,' she said, and mindful of Grant's instructions, Tamsyn allowed it to be looped over her head, murmuring her thanks.

Then, it seemed, it was time to go. After more fruit and coconut juice there came an exchange of compliments, fulsome and formal, between Grant and the chief, who then escorted them to the edge of the grass and waved them farewell as they started up the slope. At the edge of the trees Tamsyn turned to look at the village, now bustling with activity, for at least one family had opened its *umu*, and the smoky scent of cooked food hung on the air.

The sun had slipped behind the hill while they had been there; a flare pulsated orange, was joined by another, and then another until the rapidly darkening village glowed with their light. A child cried, several masculine voices sang softly, and one deluded cockerel crowed. With a sigh Tamsyn turned away. Grant took her elbow.

'It will be dark in a few minutes,' he said blandly. 'That took a little longer than I expected.'

His touch was light and impersonal, but Tamsyn was hard put to it to control her trembling. There had been no lessening of the heat with the sun's departure, but she could not suppress an involuntary shiver.

'Cold?' he asked in a voice which revealed that he knew that she wasn't.

'Always when the sun goes down.' It should have been flippant, but to her horror it sounded like an invitation.

One he wasn't slow in accepting. With a soft laugh he slipped his arm around her shoulders, drawing her close against him.

For a moment Tamsyn relaxed, then sanity prevailed and she pulled away. 'I didn't invite that,' she said stiffly. 'At least, I didn't intend to.'

'My mistake.' But he sounded amused rather than annoyed. 'I gather that Saunders decided that he had nothing to worry about from me. Or didn't you confess your sins to him?'

'Of course I did!' she flared, angry with herself for giving him an opening like this. Hot humiliation burned in her cheeks. If he had any tact at all he would not be so calmly discussing those mad feverish moments she had spent in his arms!

'Then why are you worrying? All is forgiven, I gather.'

'I don't want to talk about it.'

'Ashamed of yourself?'

Goaded beyond endurance by the taunt in his voice, she snapped,

'Yes.'

'My poor innocent! You know, your parents should never have let you loose unsuspecting on the world. Didn't your mother tell you anything beyond the bare facts of life?'

'Will you stop it?' she gritted, standing still on the path. It was dark now, the swift tropical twilight gone, and no light able to penetrate through the thick layer of foliage above them. She could not see him, but she sensed his presence with every leaping nerve of her body.

'My dear girl, I'm merely trying to make you see things in the eminently sensible way your fiancé does.'

'Leave John out of it!'

'Tamsyn, if John were out of it, I wouldn't be standing six feet away from you at the moment.' Laughter coloured his voice, adding to her fury and misery. 'Are you afraid of me?'

'I——' she stopped, caught in the trap he had set for her. If she said yes, she would be revealing her shameful attraction to him. If she said no he would deride her for her too obvious reaction to his presence.

Swallowing, she said stonily, 'I'm quite sure that you don't care in the least how I feel about you. Just leave me alone, will you?'

'Certainly.'

She heard footsteps, and knew that he had taken her at her word. For a moment she felt relief, then as she stared about her trying to see where she was, another emotion swamped her, frightening her with its intensity. Desolation, pure and simple, which made her start off up the path after him, clenching her teeth to prevent herself from crying out.

The darkness was thick and velvety, pressing against her with a choking denseness. The stream gurgled below, a quiet, soothing sound which paradoxically added to her feeling of alienation. She could not see the path, or the trees, and once blundered straight into a trunk, only protecting herself from a graze by an instinctive reaction which brought her arm up in front of her face. She stood for a long moment pressed against the smooth bark, admitting wretchedly that she could not go on.

But she would not call out to him. Although tears filled her eyes she brushed them angrily away and sat down, willing herself to relax, let the calm and peace of the night sink into her soul. After a few minutes she got up, and summoned up that knowledge which no child reared in the country is ever without, making use of unconscious memories to pick out the path. It was difficult, and several times she stumbled, but after long moments a faint lifting of the blackness revealed the edge of the jungle growth.

He was waiting for her there, a darker shadow in the darkness, and said as she came up, 'Good girl.'

'Thank you,' she said demurely, extremely pleased with herself for refusing to give in to her fears.

He laughed, and took her arm once more. 'I'm glad I wasn't mistaken about you,' he remarked with enigmatic blandness. 'Courage, and a will like steel. I hope Saunders realises just what he's taking on.'

'I'm sure he does,' she returned, infusing her voice with sweetness. 'He knows me *very* well.'

'That, my dear, is quite obvious.'

Long after Tamsyn was to remember the grimness of his voice as he said that.

'My dear, you have been working all morning! I insist that you come and drink tea with me.' Madame gazed at her guest's pale face, noting shadows beneath the green eyes. 'All yesterday, also. You are tired, I can see it. Come!'

When Madame spoke like that few disobeyed. Meekly Tamsyn followed her through the house and out on to the terrace by the drawing room. There, in the shade of a vast flame of the forest tree, was what the glossy magazines called a conversation setting: wrought iron table and comfortable lounging chairs, including a high-backed one for Madame.

The tea was refreshing and oddly cooling in the sultry heat. Served with it were small dainty cakes; at her hostess's insistence Tamsyn swallowed two of them.

'Oh, it's so *hot*!' she sighed.

'Unseasonably so. We do not have hurricanes at this time of year, but this feels like hurricane weather. How much more of this typing do you have to do?'

'Quite a bit,' Tamsyn admitted, stifling a sigh. John had sent out a great file of stuff from the engineer as well as more of his notes only that morning. With a laugh which didn't quite ring true, she continued, 'I must be infected with the lotus-eating urge. My energy seems to have run out.'

'This is not like your cooler climate, *ma petite*. You should work at a slower pace. I must have a word with that young man of yours.'

Tamsyn smiled. 'We have a deadline, Madame. Unfortunately we can't stay here for ever.'

'Ah, it is dangerous to fall in love with the tropics. They are like a disease; they thin the blood, and always there is a fever in it, a longing for heat and the sound of the trade winds in the palms. So beware, Tamsyn. Do not allow yourself to fall in love with Fala'isi.'

Tamsyn shivered, and then laughed. 'I could enjoy a brisk frost right now,' she confessed ruefully. 'If it gets any hotter I'm afraid I'll have to sink my principles and indulge in the siesta habit.'

'This afternoon, certainly you will. And a quiet night tonight. Grant will be out once more.'

Carefully Tamsyn replaced cup and saucer back on the table. Grant had gone out the last two nights; she had been relieved by his absence. When they had met he had been very aloof and cool with her, treating her with a withdrawn courtesy which should have pleased her. That it hadn't was a sign of her own foolishness, but she told herself fiercely that she was glad. The less notice she received from him the better!

And the evenings spent with Madame had been pleasant, for the older woman had travelled widely and possessed a deep and abiding interest in art and music and books, as well as being able to discuss current affairs with intelligence and enough lack of logic to make her views interesting.

'You are frowning,' Madame said quietly. 'The light is too bright, perhaps. You should wear sunglasses.'

'I will, if you don't mind.' They cut the glare, and helped hide her eyes from the two who were walking across the terrace: Grant and Liz Holland. Seeing them together gave Tamsyn a horrid hollow feeling in her stomach, but she managed to summon up a smile which she bestowed impartially on them both.

Liz collapsed gracefully into a chair, fanning herself with a wide native fan which looked too heavy for her slender wrist. 'Ohhhhh! It's so hot!' she complained. 'And this dreadful man has dragged me all over Fala'isi until I'm exhausted.'

'I shall ring for more tea,' said Madame.

But Liz pulled a face. 'Darling Mrs Chapman, do you mind if I don't? I'd like something cold and long and tinkling with ice cubes.'

One of the maids bore out a tray and set it down on the table before taking the tea tray away.

Liz beamed, 'Darling Grant—lovely!'

She was very beautiful, Tamsyn thought. Small and dainty and slim, her dark hair and eyes superbly groomed, she wore a long frock something like a Hawaian *muu-muu*, but made of exquisite embroidered cotton. Tamsyn had never found out exactly what she was doing on the island; no one had bothered to tell her and she didn't like to ask. She was English, and obviously wealthy, a member of the international circle which was the Chapmans' world, like Madame's cousin Monsieur de la Tour who was an ardent botanist and appeared only at dinner, when he was charming as ever to Tamsyn, but seemed preoccupied.

'... so I told Grant that I'd had enough, and he angelically brought me home,' Liz finished.

'You have no stamina,' Grant teased, raising his glass to her in a gesture which was a toast.

Liz laughed. 'Don't say that! I suppose the days when we could plead fragility and be cared for are long past. We should be like Miss Forsythe here, brisk and competent and useful as well as ornamental.'

A faint flush touched the pale skin beneath Tamsyn's sunglasses, but her voice was amused and rueful. 'I'm afraid I feel none of those things at the moment.'

'Is the heat getting you down too?' Liz turned to Grant. 'Remember Singapore, and how hot it was there? Like living in a steam laundry. You would hate the real tropics, Miss Forsythe, although some people become acclimatised fairly quickly.' The dark eyes turned back to Tamsyn, surveying her with what could have been mockery—it was hard to tell. 'You do look pale.'

Tamsyn felt pale, and on edge. Grant had not looked at her since he sat down, but she could feel his sardonic appraisal and wanted desperately to get away from him.

That hollow feeling had turned into something more active and painful, a gnawing of frustration and despair that increased whenever Liz Holland slanted her warm possessive eyes towards him.

'The heat,' she said lightly, getting to her feet. 'If you'll excuse me, I have work to do.'

But back in her room she stood for long moments staring down at her hands, before she took the cover from the typewriter again.

It became unbearably hot and humid. After a tray lunch on the terrace, as everyone else was out, Tamsyn showered and climbed into a cotton *muu-muu* she had bought; long and loose and brightly coloured, it was cool, but when she tried to read, the print danced before her eyes, giving her a headache, so after a few minutes she gave in and stretched out on the bed, hoping that sleep would put an end to the turmoil within her.

She woke to the crash of thunder, followed by a downpour so torrential that she lay bewildered for a moment. The french doors had been closed, no doubt by a weather-wise maid, but even through the heavy stone walls she could hear the drumming of the rain. It was dark; as she watched, lightning split the sky with brilliant savagery and there was a further roll of thunder. It was still intensely hot.

Looking at her watch, she was surprised to find that it was almost five o'clock. Soon it would be dusk, but it could hardly become any darker. Restlessly she rose and moved across to the window. During her stay on the island there had been rain, but nothing like this riot of the elements. Shivering, she realised just how terrifying the summer hurricanes must be. Yet there was something about the savagery outside that appealed to a wild streak within her. Even as a child the elemental drama of a storm had touched a sensitive chord. She stayed for a long time watching the play of the lightning, the eeriness of the garden lit by the harsh streaks of flame, the superb disregard of the weather for any of man's puny little works.

A tap on the door heralded one of the maids, Vatatera, grinning broadly.

'You OK?' she asked cheerfully.

'Yes, I'm fine, thank you.'

'Good. Mrs Chapman rang up before the storm broke to say she and Monsieur de la Tour have decided to stay to dinner at the Griegs'. She wanted to talk to you, but when

she heard you were asleep she wouldn't let me wake you.
She sent her love, and said you were to go to bed early.'

Tamsyn smiled. 'Thank you.'

'Where do you want your dinner?'

'I'll have it in here, if that's all right.'

'Yes, sure. I'll bring it down when it's ready.'

The maid cast a quick glance around the room. 'You'll be
in the dark soon. There's no need to worry about electricity.
When the power goes we've got our own generator. The
phone is out, of course.'

Tamsyn bent and touched the switch on a lamp, moving
away as it flowered into brilliance. 'How long will this
last?'

'Oh, could be all night. It will get cooler towards the
end. Can I get you something?'

'No, thank you.'

'OK. Ring if you want anything.'

She left. Tamsyn smiled as the door closed behind her.
The servants here were far from subservient, but extremely
obliging. Their affection for the Chapmans was very real
and although there was little formality in the house their
immense natural dignity made them as formal when necessary as any English servant could have been. In many ways
the Chapmans lived like the lords of old, surrounded by
luxury and waited on by willing retainers, but like those
aristocrats, their responsibilities were great. Tamsyn knew
of Madame's interest in schooling and welfare, her help to
all who came for it, as well as her cool brain which made
sure that no one put anything across her. She knew her
islanders, she had once said, adding with a twinkle, 'And
they know me!' Few who came were sent away empty-
handed, but it was not a relationship of master-servant, for
the islanders were a proud, independent people; the regard

they had for the Chapmans had been earned over the years. And it was not confined to the people of their village.

John had realised this far sooner than Tamsyn. From the first he had known that to succeed his survey must have Grant's approval. Almost Tamsyn wished that he was not so clear-thinking, for it was this instinctive appraisal of the situation which had made him so determined to have her close to Grant. And so he had put her into danger, refusing to admit that there was any.

She bit her lip. Should she have told him just what she had felt in Grant's arms, the overwhelming desire to surrender which had rendered her almost unable to resist his dark attraction? She had tried, but John had been so—so *sensible* about things! Just as Grant predicted, she remembered.

She sat down, as a new and unpleasant thought struck her with sickening clarity. In her innocence, if that was what you called such stupidity, she had assumed that Grant had kissed her because he wanted her, but why had she not realised sooner that self-control was as strongly marked in his features as the sensuality which made his embraces so exciting?

Humiliation darkened her eyes. Oh, but she was a fool, an idiot, to fall headlong into the snare he had set for her feet! No doubt there was an element of casual lust in his embraces, but there must have been much more of calculation, a ruthless test to discover just what sort of person he was dealing with in her and through her in John. A clever man, John had called him, and yet he had not comprehended more than a part of Grant's cleverness.

Painfully, the memories abhorrent to her, she set herself to recalling each incident right from the beginning, from that dance he had forced on her when he had made it so clear that she was as transparent to him as a pane of window glass. He must have understood the reason why John was so pleased by Madame's invitation, known exactly what had prompted the younger man's acceptance of it, just as he had seen Tamsyn's reluctance and drawn his own conclusions from it. And what they were she dreaded to think!

Oh, he had been clever, feeding her scraps of information, testing her with that kiss in the swimming pool, and then testing her further by the waterfall, knowing that she would tell John. The memory of the way he had talked on that ride back came clearly to her mind; more comments on his hopes and plans for the island! And John had fallen right into his trap, subduing jealousy for the sake of ambitions, refusing to admit to her or himself that there were some things no man should accept from another, the fondling of his fiancée being one of them.

Tamsyn looked down of her clenched fists, caught in the kind of desperation she had never thought to endure. They had each used her to test the other, regardless of her emotions and needs. Oddly enough it was Grant's duplicity which hurt the most. Reluctantly, painfully, she admitted to herself that she had always known that John's love was not the great passion she had dreamed of in her romantic youth when all things seemed possible.

But she had not wanted it to be! It seemed that her thoughts must be uttered aloud, so intensely did she feel the truth of them. She wanted a calm, peaceful love, like her parents' deep affection for each other, not the turbulence and terror of romance, not the thunder in her blood which Grant Chapman evoked in her by his most casual touch or merely by his presence.

The inner demon of her thoughts drove her to her feet,

setting her pacing restlessly around the darkened room. Outside the rain drummed against the glass, as merciless as the thoughts which intruded into her brain, mocking her with their refusal to be dismissed. She stopped by the typewriter, but the thought of working sickened her, and she resumed her aimless walking, aware that her hands were twisting together in the classic gesture of a distraught woman. It was still sticky hot so that she felt as though she was moving through a steam bath, and when the maid brought a tray along it was all she could do not to feel physically ill.

Starving herself would not do anybody any good. With the strong practicality which was an essential part of her character she forced down food which tasted like sawdust in her mouth. The storm rolled and crashed, lightning flaming into the room even as the rain intensified. She had heard of tropical downpours, but this was incredible! Sparing a thought for the villagers in their thatched *fales*, she took the tray along to the kitchen, exchanged a few pleasant remarks with the large amiable woman who prepared the superb meals and went back to her room. Never had she felt so lonely; forsaken was the word which sprang to mind, only to be banished hurriedly.

Forsaken she was not! John still loved her in his way as much as he was capable of loving anyone. It had once been enough for her and would be again when she had banished this infatuation of the senses which held her in thrall. She would be happy again, and wiser too. It should not be too difficult to stay out of Grant's way, as lately he seemed to have decided to ignore her.

Liz Holland's lovely, satisfied face mocked her, and with it came that nameless emotion which now revealed itself to be ugly jealousy. Tamsyn sighed, pushing a hand through her hair and refused to allow it to become more than a nagging ache. She would *not* give in to this infatuation in any way. She was still pledged to John; his blindness to anything but his own ambitions hurt but did not really surprise her. At least he was honest, for he had made no pretence about his reasons for wanting her to stay at the plantation. Subconsciously she had always known that his love was rooted deep in practicality, but it was likely to be truer for that, she thought defiantly. Love which grew of friendship must be a stronger and better emotion than this desire of the eyes and body which Grant roused in her, weakening her principles, encouraging her to be false to the vows she had made. If she could only hang on to her wits until Fala'isi was behind them, everything must come right again and Grant Chapman would recede to become no more than a memory of madness.

CHAPTER SIX

By ten o'clock Tamsyn gave up any idea of seeing Madame or Grant home that night. No one with any sense would venture out in weather like this unless there was a strong and pressing reason for it!

Vatatera reinforced this when she appeared at the door to ask if Tamsyn wanted a drink before bed.

'No, they'll stay where they are,' she said cheerfully. 'Madame, she's lived here long enough to know that it's stupid going out in a rain, and Grant will be quite happy at Miss Holland's place.' She grinned and winked broadly, her implication plain.

Jealousy seared through Tamsyn's nerves, but she kept her voice light and cool as she asked, 'Where does Miss Holland live?'

'In the town. Her father is one of the advisers to the Government. From the United Nations, I think.' The kind dark eyes surveyed Tamsyn's face keenly. 'You don't want to be frightened, miss. This is just a little storm. We're used to them here.'

'I keep thinking of the villages,' Tamsyn confessed.

The maid laughed. 'Don't you worry about them! Those *fales*, they're built for this. No rain will get through the thatch, and they'll have all the mats rolled down, so they'll be dry inside. And they're up high off the ground, so no water can get in even if it floods. No, don't you worry. I'll bring you some chocolate and you can get yourself off to bed. I've turned the air-conditioning on, so it will be cooler soon, and when you wake up in the morning the sky will be clear and the sun shining.'

The drink helped; so did the air-conditioning. Tamsyn had another shower, pulled on her nightgown, and sat down in the chair with an historical novel from the bookshelf, ready to lose herself in a fortified castle just after the time of William the Conqueror.

Much later, when the room had cooled sufficiently to make the bed look attractive, she raised her head and yawned. The rain still streamed down but there had been no lightning for some time, so it seemed that the centre of the storm had passed over. The sound of the rain would make a pleasant lullaby and the book had calmed her mind sufficiently to make sleep seem possible.

And then the door opened and Grant stood there, frowning, his hair still wet though smooth, as though he had combed it after a shower.

Tamsyn gaped. 'What—I thought you were staying out!'

'I came home,' he said flatly. His eyes raked her slender form.

She bit her lip, and looked around for a wrap, cursing the carelessness which had made her leave it off. It lay over a chair by the bathroom door; she felt as though she was treading on coals as she walked over and drew it on, pulling the cord tight as some sort of protection against him.

'I shouldn't have thought that the roads would be passable,' she managed to say.

He shrugged. 'I'm used to it. My grandmother is still at the Griegs', I take it.'

'I—yes.' Tucking her fingers beneath the cord of her robe, she swung towards him. 'She rang before, but I was asleep. She'd decided to stay to dinner. Vatatera told me she would stay the night.'

'Good.' Almost as though he had a right to be there he moved across to the uncurtained windows to look out into the night. 'This should be over by morning.' A swift, probing glance took in the tall slim figure across the room, virginal in the white robe, her slender legs and bare feet poised for flight. 'Were you frightened?'

'N-no ... No,' she said more strongly. 'It was unpleasantly hot, but we do have downpours like this back home. They just don't last so long.' Please go, she urged silently, feeling a suffocating warmth in her throat. He must have changed since he came home, for he wore slacks and a thin cotton shirt which emphasised the breadth of his shoulders. 'I'm fine,' she continued desperately, hoping that he would stop looking at her with such unsmiling concentration and leave before the tension in the room was snapped by some unforgivable act on her part.

'Good.'

He turned towards the door. Tamsyn's breath came softly through her lips, but she smiled. 'Thank you for coming
to check up on me,' she said lightly.

'It wouldn't be the first time.'

He smiled at the wave of colour which washed over the
fine skin, lightly kissed by the sun's warmth. With studied
calm she returned, 'I must remember to put my light off
earlier.'

'Because I construe it as an invitation?'

'Do you?' it was stupid to allow herself to be drawn into
this kind of conversation, but she was mesmerised by the
look in his eyes as the cold grey became warmed by leaping
fires.

'You are the invitation,' he said softly, and began to walk
towards her purposefully, yet with gait so lithe that his feet
made no sound on the green and apricot tiles.

The spell broke. Tamsyn pulled her hands from beneath
her belt and said harshly, 'No! I won't be used to ease your
frustrations! Leave me alone.'

Her hands came up to push him away, but he grasped her
by the wrists, holding her at arms' length while his eyes
probed the pallor of her face.

'Liz doesn't frustrate me,' he said coolly, ironically.
'She's a generous woman, unlike you.'

Jealousy and a bitter envy stabbed her, but she lifted her
head proudly, meeting the cynical comment with a coolness
she was far from feeling.

'The first night I was here you said that Madame had
brought me here for my protection,' she stated coldly,
implacably. 'I suppose I should think it a mark in your
favour that you waited until she was out of the house before ...'

'Before I seduced you,' he interrupted. 'That was what

you were going to say, Tamsyn, so why hesitate like a modest young virgin? I refuse to believe that you've been engaged to John Saunders for six months and not compromised your principles.'

'Why not be frank? Just say what you mean.'

'Very well, then.' He smiled and released her, then in a gesture as contemptuous as it was disturbing, touched the place on her breast where her heart beat tumultuously. 'You respond very ardently to kisses, my dear, so ardently that it's quite obvious that you've slept with your John.'

Sick at heart, she turned away, flinging over her shoulder, 'You said yourself that I'm not a generous woman. You were right, apparently, if by that you mean that I don't distribute my favours to anyone who comes by.'

Grant laughed, and drew her back against him. She could feel the regular beat of his heart driving into her shoulders, knew bitterly that her surmisal about his reasons was quite correct. She disturbed him not at all! That monotonously smooth heartbeat was all the proof she needed, for her own pulses were leaping violently, almost suffocating her. Now as never before she needed a clear head, because his purpose was frighteningly obvious. Some deep instinct told her that to resist him physically would only serve to inflame him into losing his control. At all costs she must keep him talking.

'Poor Tamsyn,' he mocked, cupping her throat gently yet with enough strength to show her that he would not let her go. His fingers moved gently, sensuously across the soft skin, resting for a long perilous moment on the fluttering pulse which betrayed her.

'Tamsyn,' he said softly, and bent his head to kiss the angle between throat and shoulder.

For a moment her physical needs played the traitor. The

desire to give in, to allow herself to be borne unresisting on this primitive tide of need, made her draw in her breath sharply, almost turn to him, but she knew a moment's sanity and thought of the shame which would be her portion after the night's madness was past.

Slowly, stiffly, she moved away, twisting John's ring on her finger as she looked at him with agonised appeal in the shadowed depths of her eyes.

'You're afraid,' he said quietly. 'Why, Tamsyn? I'm not some young fool who'll hurt you.'

Sudden tears sparkled on her lashes. 'You see everything from the physical angle,' she whispered. 'Please go, Grant. I can't take much more of this.'

Something like derision twisted his lips as he pulled her against him, resting his cheek on the bright fall of her hair.

'No—I'm not going to try anything,' he said sharply as she resisted. 'I told you once before that I'm no rapist. Is it loyalty that holds you back, because I know you're not frigid?'

'You test me all the time.' It was heaven to lie against his chest, cradled in his arms. A great sense of peace flooded into her. In a muffled voice she went on, 'I don't understand you.'

'Or yourself,' he said bleakly, as he put her away from him. 'Poor Tamsyn!'

His mockery tore at her heart, but beyond a flicker of her lashes she gave no sign that the taunt had struck home. It was suddenly very cold; outside the rain had stopped, but a wind followed hard on it, keening mournfully at the eaves. Tamsyn shivered, pulling her robe closer to her, suddenly exhausted.

'You'd better get some sleep,' Grant said, his impersonal tones making nothing of the fact that he had been trying to seduce her only a few minutes ago. 'I'll turn in myself. Not,' he went on with a cynical smile, 'with you. Goodnight.'

'Goodnight.'

When he had gone she took the robe off, allowing it to slip through nerveless fingers to the floor as she walked across to the bed. The silk sheets were warm to her skin, infinitely luxurious. In a few moments she drifted off to sleep.

The public services on the island were efficient, Tamsyn thought bleakly, as she lifted the receiver. Or perhaps Grant Chapman's line got preferential treatment!

'Everything OK?' John's voice enquired breezily. Without waiting for an answer he continued, 'Listen, love, we've been invited to a "do" at the Prime Minister's residence tomorrow night. An informal get-together, by the looks of it.'

Tamsyn frowned. Caught in the never-ending treadmill of her conscience, she found it hard to concentrate on anything.

'. . . spoken to Chapman, and he says he'll bring you in,' John was rattling on. 'I'll take you home, of course. Wear something modest, sweetie. You'll be there as my fiancée, not as my secretary, but we don't want you too conspicuous, and I notice that it's only the tourists who go in for the outrageous. How's the work coming on?'

'The work? Oh, fine, fine.'

'Good, because there's a stack here for you. We've been busy while you do your lotus-eating.' He laughed.

Tamsyn echoed it obediently. Lotus-eating! 'I'll send it out this morning. Bye, darling. See you tomorrow night.'

'John——' But he had already hung up. Tamsyn stood

looking down at the receiver for a long, frowning moment, then turned to see Grant's secretary, the pleasant, self-effacing Mr Tolman who lived alone in a small cottage in the grounds, standing beside her.

She summoned up a smile for him.

'You look a bit tired. Is the heat getting you down? It can be dynamite if you're not used to it.'

'It was awful last night,' Tamsyn evaded. 'It seems incredible that we should have had such a terrific storm when you look outside.'

'Yes, I suppose so.' He joined her at the window. Apart from one gardener, who was busy tying up some strands of a creeper which had broken loose, there was no sign of the torrential downpour except for a crisp freshness in the air. The brilliant silken flowers of the hibiscus bushes glowed like jewels in a green crown, the poinciana was a scarlet parasol with a crimson carpet beneath it.

'Everything smells much fresher after a rain,' the secretary said, then, with a smile, 'Well, talking won't get my work done. Like you, I've a lot to do. Grant leaves in a couple of days for America, and woe betide me if I haven't got him all clued up.'

Tamsyn took a deep breath, fighting for control. 'How sweet the frangipani smells,' she commented swiftly. 'Are you going with him, Mr Tolman?'

'Oh yes. But like you, I won't be having a holiday. Four days of high-pressure business talks will keep me busy. He was going for a week, but he's decided to cut back on the number of days he's away. I'll arrive back feeling as though I've been run over, and he'll be as fresh as a daisy. He doesn't tire easily, which is just as well, since he has a demanding life.'

'It seems a very pleasant life,' Tamsyn returned drily,

thinking of the hours Grant spent with Liz Holland.

'He works harder than he plays. Fortunately he's extremely efficient.'

'I suppose it's a matter of having to be.' Tamsyn turned away from the window, aware that he was keen to get back to his work, and that she, too, had work to do.

But once out in the corridor she met Madame, just returned from her overnight stay.

'Ah, Tamsyn, I am so *sorry*,' the older woman said urgently, her slim hand touching Tamsyn's affectionately. 'I should never have stayed once the rain began, but like a fool I allowed myself to be persuaded.'

Was it imagination, or did those dark, deep-set eyes scan her face anxiously, as though searching for signs of—what? As she reassured Mrs Chapman, Tamsyn told herself that she was being absurdly sensitive, and indeed, Madame seemed to relax almost immediately, becoming her brisk self once more.

'Come, let us go for a walk to inspect the damage,' she decided, stripping off her gloves. 'Grant told me that there is little to see here, but he has already rung around to see if any district needs help. And now he flies to the other side of the island to check there, also.'

'Flies, Madame?'

'He has a small plane kept at the airport. He is a good pilot, so I do not worry—much.'

Tamsyn laughed and went around the garden with Madame on her arm. You had to admire her indomitable spirit, she thought, as the thin black-clad figure issued crisp orders to a boy weeding one of the beds. Madame ran this huge place so well that one was never conscious of the many hours of effort it needed from both staff and owner to keep it immaculate, she was a gracious and clever hostess, and she had all of her outside interests as well. Not an easy task for a woman well into her seventies, but Madame gave no sign of being unequal to the demands made upon her by all of those who loved her.

'Fortunately the soil is volcanic,' she was saying now. 'It is very free-draining, which means that one must be careful of erosion. The Polynesians live so much in harmony with nature that they interfere with it very little, but one must watch the newcomers, who do not always understand. Or care, for many of them see only that their profits are being lessened by our very strict planning laws. Fortunately our Council is very sensible, and they love Fala'isi.'

'Who wouldn't?' Tamsyn said softly.

'Yes, it is easy to love. Some young people find life here dull. Miss Holland, for one.' The wise old face crinkled into sly laughter. 'I do not think she would remain here if it were not for the fact that Grant makes it his headquarters.'

Well, that made abundant sense; Tamsyn had known it ever since that first night. Now she would like very much to ask Madame what she thought the situation was between her grandson and the glamorous Liz, but of course she couldn't, and to be quite frank she didn't really want to know. At the moment she had herself well in hand, all emotions damped down. If she didn't allow them free rein she might perhaps get through the next couple of days until Grant left for the States, and then there would be a merciful breathing space when she would be able to reassemble the shattered parts of her life and patch them up until she got back to New Zealand. Once there, she knew bleakly, there would come a time of reckoning when she would have to examine her whole relationship with John to see if it was worth salvaging. But that could wait. At the moment she must live from day to day.

Mid-morning brought the arrival of some cousin of Madame's from Tahiti with his three daughters, girls with the exquisite chicness of the French grafted on to the superb physical beauty of Polynesia. They were gay and laughing and totally without inhibitions, kissing Madame and Tamsyn impartially, joking with the staff in a language which was close enough to that of the islanders to be mutually understandable and laughing, the rich sound of it enlivening the big house as they unpacked their clothes in adjoining bedrooms.

They had come across in one of the big cruise ships and described their impact on the male part of the ship's complement with much gaiety, while their father, a tall, stooped, thin man with vague eyes and a wistful smile, looked on benignly. They were like beautiful, exotic flowers, with their dark eyes and long black hair, their graceful movements and mellow voices which seemed more often than not to sing the words. When Monsieur de la Tour arrived home from his botanising they greeted him with the same enthusiastic welcome they had lavished on Madame.

He disengaged himself and came over to Tamsyn, smiling. 'How do you like our birds of paradise?' he asked with twinkling eyes. 'One would think that after boarding school and a very strict French finishing school they would be a little more restrained, no?'

The girls laughed, and the oldest, Solange, protested, 'But, *mon cousin*, we can be very restrained! Look! Yvette, Marie!'

Their curtsies were the epitome of primness, the gesture with which each held out her hand, dignified in the extreme.

Monsieur de la Tour flung up his hands. 'Ah, I admit it!

But I prefer a bouquet of flowers to three stiff dowagers! Tell me, beautiful ones, how long do you stay with us?'

'For three days.' Solange seemed to be spokeswoman for the sisters. 'Then we fly to Paris to buy my trousseau. Are you coming to my wedding, *mon cousin*?'

'But of course. Tahiti in the spring is delightful.' He turned to Tamsyn, 'This little one marries an American and will live in Hawaii with him.'

Solange accepted Tamsyn's good wishes with unaffected pleasure, glancing at John's diamond as she said 'You, also, are betrothed. When is your day of happiness, *m'selle*?'

'We haven't set the day yet,' Tamsyn spoke awkwardly, angry with herself for being upset by the wondering look in the huge dark eyes. But Solange was polite, and nodded.

'One cannot always follow the promptings of one's heart and fly into marriage like the birds,' she observed sagely. 'Papa insisted that my Pierre and I wait for a year so that we might know our own hearts truly. I stayed at Hawaii with his parents to see if I loved his family enough to live close to them. They live on Oahu on a big cattle ranch.'

'And you liked them?'

Solange nodded vigorously. 'Oh, very much, and they liked me, also. In Hawaii they do not mind if one has Polynesian blood. It is not always so. Also Papa has given me a large dowry.'

She sounded very down-to-earth about the whole affair. Tamsyn blinked, then realised that here was an example of the rock-hard practicality of both France and Polynesia. Solange loved her Peter, but she was also sensible enough to realise that her heritage could have caused difficulties with his family. How anyone could dislike such a lovely girl was almost beyond Tamsyn, but no doubt if there had been any hesitation on their part Papa's generosity would have alleviated it. And once she had stayed with them they would love her.

Grant arrived home almost at dusk, and was enveloped in soft golden arms and requests for kisses. An unwilling spectator, Tamsyn saw his narrowed eyes gleam with laughter as he kissed each tempting mouth. There was no doubt that the Polynesian's frank regard for sexual attraction was not repressed in these girls. As Solange observed softly:

'Grant, if I did not love my Pierre to distraction I would try very much to compromise you into marrying me. You are a man!'

Whereupon her sisters made assenting noises, and Grant laughed. 'So is Peter Hubsch, my bird of paradise.'

'But of course.' Solange looked dreamily at her cousin and sighed. 'I feel an ache for him—here,' she announced, pressing her hand into her breast.

'Not much longer now, *chérie*. We will all dance at your wedding with light hearts.' He looked across at Tamsyn.

Something in the quality of that intent look made Tamsyn catch her breath. This was a new Grant, teasing and yet kind, but there was no kindness in the smile he gave her. It was almost as if he forced himself to acknowledge her presence. In a mocking voice he observed, 'One white rose in a bouquet of hibiscus blossoms.'

Solange looked swiftly at Tamsyn, her expression enquiring. 'An English rose, I think. But those eyes are not at all English, so green and dark-lashed. The English have pale eyes.'

'What do you know of the English?' Grant asked derisively.

A wicked glance from Solange made him laugh once more. 'No—don't tell me,' he said, 'I'd rather not know.

I'll bet my cousin is looking forward to the day when he has you all safely married.'

Their father smiled fondly at his beautiful vivid daughters. 'They are good girls, my little ones, and the house will be empty when they go.'

Instantly there was a chorus of protests, Yvette assuring him that it would be many years yet before they all left him, her voice very warm and loving as she spoke.

Tamsyn watched them a little wistfully, suddenly homesick. It took an effort of will to banish it and talk to Monsieur de la Tour, who was interested in telling her about a rare fern he had discovered that morning. The conversation became general. Grant told his mother that the storm had wrought little damage and that easily repairable. Within a few minutes there was sherry; shortly afterwards Liz Holland arrived, elegant in a stunning outfit of dark ruby silk jersey which emphasised her tiny, desirable figure.

It was an odd situation, Tamsyn thought from her vantage point beside Monsieur de la Tour. Liz had looked startled at the sight of the three Gascoigne girls, but recovered herself swiftly and proceeded to make it quite clear that she considered herself to have some claim on Grant, her slender fingers clinging to his sleeve as he performed the introductions.

As always she was gracefully deferential to Madame, and to the two elderly men, ignoring Tamsyn (also as usual) except for a smile tossed across the room, but when Grant left the room she allowed a faint patronising note to creep into her voice as she spoke to the girls.

Tamsyn squirmed, but was somewhat reassured by the wicked glint of amusement in Solange's great dark eyes. Sure enough, within a few minutes all three girls had resumed what Monsieur de la Tour had referred to as their dowager manner, becoming three sophisticated French-women. Almost Tamsyn applauded as chagrin became apparent in Liz's expression. It deepened when Grant came back, darkly resplendent in white dinner jacket and scarlet cummerbund, the formal dinner wear all over the island, and was mobbed—in the most ladylike fashion—by his cousins. The Gascoigne sisters resented being patronised and they were kind as well as perceptive, for within a few minutes they had swept Tamsyn into their orbit too and proceeded to give the evening the atmosphere of a gala occasion while their elders looked indulgently on, Grant the most indulgent of all.

Madame must have done some rapid ringing up and organising, because they sat down twenty to dinner, and there were several young men, obviously invited for the lovely sisters. John was not there.

After the meal Madame explained, 'I tried to contact Mr Saunders, but he was not at the hotel and had left no instructions for reaching him. I am sorry, my child.'

'It doesn't matter,' Tamsyn murmured, conscious that it did matter.

'You are a good, sensible child,' Madame returned understandingly, patting her hand. 'We go now down to the village. They wish to welcome my cousin and his daughters.'

They all went down in cars, leaving them parked some hundred yards away from the little valley. Flares lit the way through the palms, the flickering flames bestowing yellow light on the guests. At the grassy edge of the square a group of people waited; as Grant led his party into sight they burst into song, dancing what was obviously a welcome. Tamsyn felt something grip her by the throat at the sight of the bronzed oiled bodies, the fluttering movements of the women's hands, the immense dignity of the group of old men who waited regal as kings for their guests. The same feeling must have kept the beautifully gowned women and their escorts silent when the dance ended; no one applauded or whispered.

The chief spoke, extending a greeting as formalised as a ritual at any court. Grant replied, and then formality was gone, and there was laughter as they were urged towards a wide sandy place where mats had been spread. Mindful of Grant's instructions, Tamsyn sat cross-legged in the place assigned to her. A quick glance showed that everyone else had followed suit, Liz Holland pouting as she manoeuvred herself down. Madame was given a wide stool beside one of the girls from the village, a pretty thing with sadness in her dark eyes, who seemed to have a place of honour.

'The village virgin,' the young man beside her said softly as he noticed the direction of Tamsyn's glance. 'She is sad because her father has arranged for her to marry a young man from across the island and she does not want to.'

Tamsyn looked her amazement. 'Will she have to?'

'Oh, yes. She is a very important person and will cement ties between the families. It wouldn't occur to her to refuse, but she is not happy about it.'

The sound of singing captured their attention and for a while Tamsyn forgot the girl and her unhappiness, forgot even her own torment of mind and body. A group of children seemed to appear from the sea, singing like angels, their dark eyes gleaming in the light of the flares. Long *leis* of flowers hung from their necks, their hands moved with sinuous grace as they danced and sang, then retreated in wave-like movements back across the short turf.

The young men followed; their movements were energetic, almost threatening as they postured and leaped to the insistent rhythm of the wooden drums, and then the women, graceful and gleaming, their mellow voices seductive as they swayed.

Movement around her made Tamsyn drag her homesick eyes from the performers. The *puhi*, the virgin, had risen, and with her the Gascoigne girls, who should have looked incongruous in their dinner dresses, but as each kicked her shoes off and swayed on to the dancing floor their Polynesian heritage became strikingly apparent. At first they joined the women who were already there, then as the beat of the drums quickened the visitors launched into a real Tahitian *hula*, their hips moving so quickly that they should have become dislocated, while their hands made smooth, undulating movements like swallows over the meadows.

Softly at first, then more loudly, the onlookers began to clap to the rhythm. Tamsyn was not surprised when more visitors rose to their feet, because the atmosphere was electrically stimulating. She remembered the twenty-first birthday party of a friend of hers on the *marae* at home, and felt once more the pangs of homesickness, then felt herself pulled to her feet and joined in with the rest of them.

Much later, after Yvette had given up trying to teach a group of them the exact movements of the stomach muscles which produced that rapid hip movement of the *hula*, Tamsyn left the laughing group and made her way back to where Madame sat smiling benignly as she talked to several of the older women.

'Ah, you have exhausted yourself,' Madame greeted her. 'I do not ask if you have enjoyed yourself doing it!'

Tamsyn gave her a brilliant smile, half drugged by the festive atmosphere and weariness.

'It's been marvellous, but I've run out of energy.'

'They will dance all night,' the chief's large wife said, adding with a chuckle, 'Once I would have joined them, but I am too fat now.'

Tamsyn sat with her legs curled beneath her, watching through half-closed eyes the uninhibited movements of the dancers as they swayed to the throbbing of the log drums. The Gascoigne sisters were thoroughly enjoying themselves, their serene faces laughing and gay while around them the villagers and the young people from the islands danced too in the glow of the flares. Children danced, then dropped, then danced again, their natural grace and sense of time perfect. Tamsyn looked keenly among the agile throng for one particular figure, but Grant was not there. A moment later she saw him talking to the chief. Someone must have said something amusing, for his teeth gleamed in a smile. A small child came running from the darkness, flung his arms around Grant's leg and said something. He bent and picked the child up. The little black head rested confidingly against his lean cheek as one chubby arm curled around his neck. Tamsyn realised that she loved Grant Chapman, completely, irrevocably and hopelessly.

CHAPTER SEVEN

IT was a giggle which woke her and the depression of the side of the bed as it sank beneath someone's weight.

Tamsyn opened her eyes. Solange was laughing at her, as fresh as if she had not stayed up till three o'clock the night before, dancing the moon down.

'The colour of your brows and lashes is natural,' Solange said triumphantly. 'I knew they were! But Yvette said no, one who has such blonde hair must have pale lashes too.'

'Good morning,' Tamsyn said sleepily, smothering a yawn.

Came another enchanting giggle. 'It really is time you were awake, you know. Grant has had his breakfast and says he will wait no longer than half an hour for us.'

'Us?'

'But yes, us! Do you not remember? Last night he said he would take us riding. We go to the orchid farm.'

Tamsyn did remember. Remembered everything else too. Her mind searched swiftly for an excuse, and found the most convenient. 'You'll have to count me out,' she apologised, nodding towards the typewriter on the table. 'I've a stack of work to do.'

'Nonsense! A ride will brush away those cobwebs and turn your pale cheeks into nice pink ones.' Solange rose, darted like a humming-bird across the room and flung open the doors of the wardrobe. 'Quick! You have a shower and I will choose clothes for you to wear.'

The discovery of last night must have had some cataclysmic effect on Tamsyn's will power for she found herself obeying Solange meekly, even to climbing without demur into the jeans and thin silk shirt the other girl had chosen. Or perhaps it was because Solange was imperious, a little like Madame when the mood took her.

A tray awaited her, rolls and coffee and pineapple juice, sweetly acid and just right for chasing away any lingering lethargy.

Solange chattered, mostly about her coming wedding, but made Tamsyn jump a little when she demanded, 'What do you think of Miss Holland?'

'I—well, I hardly know her,' Tamsyn returned faintly, picking up the coffee cup to hide her face.

'I, also, but I do not like her. And she does not like me. She thinks to marry Grant.'

A knife turned slowly in Tamsyn's heart. 'They seem well suited.'

'Do you think so?' Solange opened her eyes to their widest extent. '*I* do not think so. Grant is *very* much a man, masterful and proud like Lucifer. He would not choose to marry a little nobody without breeding like Miss Holland. She is beautiful, but each of Grant's *chères amies* has been beautiful, for he will have only the best.'

Tamsyn swallowed the last of her coffee, then said determinedly, 'I think you're being indiscreet.'

The long lashes fluttered down. Solange was silent, then said quietly, 'Perhaps, but I do not think that you are, Tamsyn. And it is common knowledge that Grant has had mistresses.' She spread her hands in a purely Gallic gesture, 'He is a man whom women love—too much.'

By now Tamsyn had a firm grip on herself. 'I believe you,' she said drily, getting to her feet. 'But if you don't want him tearing up the turf because we're late, I suggest we go. The half hour is up.'

Sugar was her mount again, as she had been before. As they rode quietly through the palms Tamsyn wondered rather drearily how time could go so swiftly—and so slowly. It seemed as though she had lived all of her life at the plantation, yet counted by days she had spent such a short time there. She had been happy, almost carefree, serene in the contentment of her love. And now that love had gone as if it had never existed, as perhaps it never had. Whatever emotions she had felt for John paled into noth-

ingness compared with the turbulent, all-consuming fire
that enveloped her being now.

Last night's revelation of her true feelings for Grant had
been shattering, as shattering as that last thing she had seen
before she went to bed. It had been hot and she had turned
off the lamp, then walked across to the windows, loath to
make the final commitment of crawling between the sheets.
And had seen Grant and Liz on the lawn, their bodies
blended together into one shadow in the moonlight as they
kissed. For a moment she had stared at them, then feeling
like a Peeping Tom, she had turned and blindly groped her
way through the room, her heart breaking into agony. It
had been long before she slept, and even then it was to
dream horrible nightmares in which she was chained so that
she could not move while all around her a grinning circle of
people pointed and laughed at her helplessness.

Things did not seem so bad this morning. Tamsyn
smiled wryly as she thought that if life had taught her
nothing else it had taught her that nothing ever seemed
quite so bad in the morning as it did in the small hours.

'Something amuses you?'

Her pulse leaped before settling into a beat much faster
than usual. Grant had dropped back to beside her and was
viewing her with an intent, rather taunting glance. That
erratic organ, her heart, seemed to contract at the sight of
him, but she refused to do more than slant him a sideways
glance.

'I was thinking about the children last night,' she answered. 'They looked so charming, so totally absorbed in the
dancing.'

'You did quite well yourself. Presumably you enjoyed the
affair?'

'Yes, I did.'

She could tell by the sound of his voice that he was smiling.

'You look like the morning after the night before,' he commented.

This time she did look at him, indignation flaming into life in her expression.

'I thought that would bring your head up,' he teased, 'There's something very off-putting about talking to the top of someone's head. And the shadows under your eyes are very appealing. They give you a deceptive air of fragility.'

There could be no reason other than common courtesy for him to pay her any attention, but the contrast between his cold refusal to acknowledge her presence over the past few days and the gentle mockery in his voice and expression now was filling Tamsyn with a dangerous delight. He looked confident and wickedly attractive, with the sun striking blue sparks from his hair and the amused smile that softened the cruel line of his lips.

'Well, thank you,' she retorted crisply, while something within her woke into vibrant life. 'I'll remember that, if I ever need to impress someone with my fragility. A swift smear of eyeshadow and I'll bring out everyone's protective instincts!'

A lazy gleam of laughter warmed the grey eyes. 'It will certainly be far more attractive than the brisk competence you display most of the time. I prefer my women fragile and clinging.'

'Do you?' she mocked, greatly daring. 'I'd thought you more intelligent than that!'

He laughed and flung up a hand in acknowledgment.

'*Touché*, my girl. How do you like my little cousins?'

'Very much.' Tamsyn watched them as she spoke; they

rode very well, but a little stiffly as if well taught but not very experienced.

'Yes, I thought you would.'

He seemed disposed to say no more, so Tamsyn asked, 'Have you relatives scattered all over the Pacific?'

'An apt way of putting it. Yes, all over the world, both French and English. I must admit that these are some of the more charming.'

Tamsyn chuckled. 'You would be extraordinarily hard to please if you expected more charm than they have.'

'Yes, they're darlings,' he said unexpectedly, then slanted a narrow, intent glance her way. 'They think you beautiful as the dawn and not happy.'

'Oh!' Tamsyn was taken aback by the unexpectedness of this remark. For a moment she stared at him, mouth half open, then closed it firmly, her eyes sparkling with a mixture of fear and embarrassment. The Gascoigne girls might be perspicacious, but they had no tact, and she thought she knew Grant well enough by now to be aware that he said nothing without a reason.

'Are you unhappy?' he probed, refusing to be intimidated.

'Do I look unhappy?' It was an evasion and he recognised it.

Smiling sharply, he said, 'How should I know? I don't study your expression with such intentness that I can pretend to know every emotion that shows itself in the green depths of your eyes. But if you pressed me, I would hazard a guess that something has upset your equilibrium. It might, of course, be the fact that you're pining for your lover. It's three days, isn't it, since you've seen him? Or it could be that you've discovered a shift in your own emotions, and are not quite certain of how to cope with it?'

Never in her life had Tamsyn been more relieved by an interruption than she was when Solange turned her horse and cantered back towards them, her clear call breaking into the cocoon of tension which Grant had created by the accuracy of that last remark.

Tamsyn forced herself to respond to Solange's chatter, but a cold fear she could not banish made itself felt deep within her. Did Grant realise what had happened to her? Dear God, he could not know that she had fallen head over heels in love with him; surely she had shown no sign of it, surely, even in the long moment when he had looked across the dancers at the village and his eyes had held hers for what seemed an age. No, it was impossible! The shifting glare of the torches had prevented any close scrutiny, so her secret, so newly discovered, must be safe yet.

Yet there was more than idle conjecture or the desire to taunt in that last comment of his. Grant was not given to casual comments, and a taunt could only hurt if it hit its mark. He knows something, she thought, her suddenly tense grip setting the mare to fretting. Before Sugar could do more than take a few prancing steps sideways Grant bent to catch the bridle close by the bit, his lean fingers white at the knuckles as he forced Sugar still.

'Damn the beast!' he muttered, raking Tamsyn's startled face with a fierce glance. 'Take more care!'

Acutely conscious of Solange's curiosity, Tamsyn returned meekly, 'I'm sorry, I wasn't concentrating.'

'Keep your mind on the job in hand,' he ordered before straightening up to look arrogantly at Solange.

His cousin closed her lips firmly, lashes lowered over her eyes so that the expression in their dark depths couldn't be read. After a moment or so she said demurely, 'Where do we turn to go down to the orchid plantation, Grant?'

'Just ahead.' He called, and the two in front reined in their mounts, both laughing at some private joke.

'Here, *mes enfants*,' Grant said almost paternally, gesturing towards a wide, carefully paved way which crossed the grass. 'We follow the old road from here.'

Tamsyn asked curiously. 'This looks very old. Is it pre-European?'

'Yes,' Grant pointed towards the highest peak in the chain of mountains which formed the rugged spine of Fala'isi. 'It's the old processional way from the beach at Raroto Bay to a *marae* on Papanui, the tallest mountain. The temple of all the gods was situated as high up Papanui as they could take a road.'

Tamsyn looked down at the carefully cut and joined paving stones, and wondered just how many bare brown feet had worn them smooth as the islanders sang their way up to their temple, the home of their fierce warlike gods. Even yet, no grass pushed its way through the thin cracks between the slabs, although it was growing in from the edge.

'It's ... sad,' she murmured, her gaze following the road as it wound up the hillsides above.

'If you think that is sad you should go to Rapanui,' Solange told her quietly. 'Easter Island, you call it. Papa has been there, and he says that the great stone statues gazing forlornly across the silent grasslands awed him into silence and melancholy. Have you visited it, Grant?'

'No, that's something in store for me.' He touched Tamsyn's arm, bringing her attention back to the present day. 'If you're really interested I'll take you up higher some day. The views are magnificent.'

'I'd like that.' It was a conventional answer to a conventional gesture. He had no intention of taking her up the silent track, and she certainly wouldn't go with him if he did offer!

As they followed the track down into the dimness of the trees Solange said to Tamsyn, 'Tante Marie tells us that you go with Grant to the reception at the Prime Minister's home tonight.'

Put like that it made her flush. 'Yes, we're meeting my fiancé there,' she replied.

'He is handsome, this man of yours?'

Tamsyn smiled, 'Yes, he's very handsome.'

'Like a sun-god,' Solange mused. 'Or so Tante Marie says.' Her eyes dwelt a moment on Grant's broad shoulders. 'Interesting, is it not? You are betrothed to Apollo, yet you live in the house of Pluto. And you are silver fair yourself, like Artemis who dwelt in the moon and loved no man.'

Tamsyn laughed to hide the odd little shudder the lightly spoken words gave her. 'You speak poetically.'

'The advantages of a classical education. I was educated in the French fashion. I shall enjoy meeting this fiancé of yours tonight.'

'Are you coming with us tonight?' Tamsyn was surprised, although a moment's thought would have told her that it was hardly likely for the Government of the island to ignore Monsieur Gascoigne. He was an important official on Tahiti, as well as being Grant Chapman's relative, and even though this was a private visit the Polynesians would wish to offer their famed hospitality.

'Oh yes. It will be a little dull, but Papa has to do these things, and he likes us to go with him.'

Solange tilted her head as she gazed enquiringly at Tamsyn. 'This bewilders me, this relationship between you and your betrothed.' Her shoulders lifted in a Gallic shrug.

'Me, I could not work for my Pierre; all the time we would be making love.'

'That, *chérie*, is because you are sprung from two of the most passionate races of humanity.' That was Grant, his voice as sardonic as the gleam in his eyes. 'Tamsyn and her fiancé are of staid Northern stock; they tuck their emotions into tidy compartments, producing only the appropriate ones for the occasion. That's why Tamsyn can remain secretary to her lover, and you could not, Solange.'

'I think you are a little unfair,' Solange protested warmly, half laughing. 'You also have that staid English background, my Grant, but I do not for one moment believe that your blood is thick and cold!'

He responded to the challenge in her voice with an ironic half-bow. 'My thanks, but you're forgetting that we share a common heritage, a touch of Mediterranean sun to warm the Arctic ice of my English ancestors.'

Solange shot him a curious look before saying directly, 'Your English grandfather was no man of ice, if the family stories are to be believed. Me, I do not think for one moment that Tamsyn is a snow maiden. Look at her mouth; it is ripe as any Frenchwoman's! And those eyes are deceptively clear, I think. They hide secrets.' She eyed Tamsyn's blush with a mischievous grin then, chuckling, continued, 'And that touch of wild rose becomes your clear skin very well. I think, Grant, that you are cross with Tamsyn because she is in love with her handsome Mr Saunders and has no time for you!'

The mischief in her laughter robbed the words of any intent to hurt, but Tamsyn's blush deepened and the fleeting glance that she shot at Grant went no higher than his chin.

And he, his deep voice showing no more than lazy amusement, answered, 'Perhaps you're right, Solange. I am, of course, so conceited that I can't bear any woman to be indifferent to me.'

'Ah, do you never lose your temper?' Solange demanded cheerfully.

'Only under the most extreme provocation.'

'It is his superb self-assurance, you know,' Solange told Tamsyn in mock-confidential tones. 'He is quite impervious to anything I can think of to say to him. For years I have tried to make him just a tiny bit angry, but always he smiles as if he were my favourite uncle. It is enough to drive a woman mad! Do you not think so?'

'Tamsyn wouldn't understand a woman who is engaged to one man yet craves attention from another,' Grant interpolated coolly, before she had time to answer.

The note of mockery in his voice was cruelly obvious, so obvious that Solange looked curiously at him, and then at Tamsyn as though seeking an answer to a question which had just occurred to her. To Tamsyn's relief she said nothing, and as they had arrived at the fork in the trail where Marie and Yvette waited, and conversation became general, she was able to relax.

Listening quietly, she discovered that Grant was to accompany his uncle and cousins to the USA via Hawaii where Solange would have a rapturous reunion with her Pierre. They spoke of flying half way around the world as if it was nothing; Grant was leaving tomorrow, and yet there was none of the last-minute flurry which had marked the day before her much shorter journey to Fala'isi. The contrast between Grant, cool, completely confident, out on an expedition of pleasure and the harried thing she had been before catching the plane impressed on her once more the wide gap between their respective life styles.

These people took their wealth and their position completely for granted. Solange thought nothing of flying to Paris to shop for her trousseau. Grant lived like a feudal lord without ever giving his anachronistic way of life a passing thought.

Perhaps she was being a little unfair, for the Chapmans at least showed by their actions that they realised that the days when a man could carve out a little kingdom for himself in the South Pacific were long past. They were doing their best to bring Fala'isi into the twentieth century of democracy and independence and universal suffrage. She must give them credit for that.

But the rich were very different, she thought wryly, without envy. They even thought differently. His conversation with Solange showed that Grant felt no shame at the memory of the moments when he had made love to another man's fiancée.

An unbidden blush at those same memories made her lower her head so that no one should see what was revealed in her expression. The sun blazed down through the thin material of her shirt, and the air was moist and humid, touched with an elusive, exotic perfume which seemed to be the scent of the tropics themselves. A harsh screech signalled the arrival of exquisitely coloured parakeets, scarlet and green and blue, as vivid in their way as the Gascoigne sisters, at home in this wonderland as she could never be, Tamsyn thought sadly.

One of the girls trilled with laughter at something Grant had said; the deep tones of his voice had the power to invoke a reaction in Tamsyn so strong that it was almost physical. Her pulses raced, then steadied, and she bit her lip in helpless despair.

In some ways perhaps it would have been better if he was a conventional seducer, she thought; she could have had an affair with him, had her heart broken, and been forced to pick up the pieces of her life again, secure in the knowledge that she had loved unworthily. But at no time had he persuaded her into his arms against her will, and when her fear and shame had called a halt to their lovemaking, he had accepted her decision. Perhaps, she thought bleakly, their mutual desire was too strong to be controlled completely, but was held in check by a code of honour which did not permit the ultimate surrender.

'You look very *triste*,' Yvette remarked suddenly. 'Are you thinking of something sad?'

Tamsyn improvised rapidly. 'I'm thinking that I'll have to write to my parents soon.'

'You have parents?'

Such was her interest that Tamsyn found herself talking about her life back home. Yvette listened intently, then reinforced Tamsyn's thoughts of a few moments before by remarking, 'It is interesting to hear how you live, Tamsyn; so this is the first time you have left your country. Do you find Fala'isi very different?'

Tamsyn laughed, and explained just how different she found the island, her eyes reflective as they gazed around at the dense hibiscus jungle around them. And when they arrived at the orchid farm she could only gasp, for these orchids were like a crop, grown in fields of vivid pinks and reds, golds, blues and purples, exquisite, lush and exotic.

'Fields of butterflies,' Yvette murmured dreamily. 'Can New Zealand show a sight like that?'

'Daffodils in spring.' That was Grant, from behind. 'New Zealand's beauty is more subtle than this, Yvette, but in summer the pohutukawa trees ring the coasts with a girdle of fire.'

'One day I will go—in summer.' Yvette chuckled and threw a coquettish glance. 'I think it might be too cold for me at any other time.'

The track wound down through the fields of orchids to a complex of buildings set in a big quadrangle. Half an hour later Tamsyn felt that she knew exactly how royalty felt when being escorted around by willing and enthusiastic yet protocol-conscious guides. The Gascoigne sisters, spontaneous and outgoing though they were, had dignity of a kind that was understood by the manager of the plantation; he treated them with a courtesy which had a little of the courtier and much of the male in it. He was an islander who told Tamsyn that he had studied in Hawaii and Singapore to gain experience. His deep voice was warmly enthusiastic as he described what was being done on the plantation.

There was no doubt that it was an efficient, well-run business enterprise. Tamsyn admired vandas, cattleyas and the brilliant waxy spathes of anthuriums, listened to figures and information, and was aware of Grant's presence beside her all of the time.

When at last it was time to go, she looked rather helplessly at the exquisite lilac and gold blossom which had been presented to her with a flourish. The Gascoigne sisters tucked their huge scarlet flowers in their long black tresses, but Tamsyn's hair was too fine and silky to afford any refuge to such a fragile blossom.

It was taken from her fingers by Grant, who, with a taunting smile, inserted the stem through the buttonhole of her shirt, his fingers hard and casual against her breast. Conscious of Solange's dark glance on them, of the interest in the young manager's eyes, she forced a smile.

'Thank you,' she murmured, hating him.

'My pleasure.'

Everyone went to the reception. When they arrived back from the orchid farm it was to find that a messenger had been bearing the Prime Minister's official greetings in the true fashion of Polynesian hospitality and a formal invitation to Monsieur Gascoigne and his daughters.

Telling herself that she should not be startled at anything she discovered about this family, not even that the invitation had been addressed to Monsieur le Comte, plus a string of names, all of which seemed very aristocratic to her ears, Tamsyn looked glumly at herself in the mirror just before setting out. John had said that the reception was an informal get-together; to be on the safe side she wore a floor-length shirtwaister of softly flowing voile in pale greens and lilac which emphasised her fairness yet was modest and unobtrusive as well as becoming. Around her wrist she looped a thin gold chain; that, with pearl studs in her ears and her engagement ring, was her only jewellery.

Fully expecting to be completely overshadowed by Solange and her sisters, she discovered that she had forgotten the French heritage of elegance and restrained good taste. Three demure maidens met in the main salon before dinner, although a Polynesian touch of flamboyance was evident in the red frangipani arranged skilfully against each dark head.

The reception began formally enough. The stout, immensely dignified Prime Minister met them in the foyer of his official residence, his tall wife beside him. An aide gave their names; Tamsyn shook hands, received a smile and a shrewd look from the Minister, a wider smile and an even shrewder look from his wife.

Somewhat surprised by their interest, she moved beside Grant into a wide room, accepted a glass of white wine from a waiter in a white jacket and magnificent scarlet *sula*, the national skirt of the men of Fala'isi, and looked around for John.

The room was filled with people, islanders in their national costume, the women in long cotton sari-like gowns of the vivid colours which suited their golden-brown skins, the men in impeccably tailored jackets and shirts above their *sulas*. There were many *papalagi*, as anyone not of Fala'isi was called, but no sign of John, though Margot Henderson, the anthropologist, was there talking earnestly to a little Chinese man, and she could see the engineer away over the other side of the room. But no John.

'He must be working late.'

She cast a glittering look at Grant, reacting to the thread of mockery in his voice. 'Probably,' she returned sweetly, smiling up into his handsome face in a spirit of pure bravado.

His narrowed glance was intent and stabbing as a lance, but before he could speak John's voice said something and John was there, his blue eyes quickly taking in the members of the party, his expression alert and winning.

After that the evening passed as a kind of theatrical event for Tamsyn. There was no way that she could talk to John, nothing to do but follow his lead and watch him charm everyone in sight from the Prime Minister's wife to sixteen-year-old Marie Gascoigne. And try not to see Grant with Liz Holland. At least, she thought wearily, it was the sort of evening which forced one to circulate, so he didn't spend overmuch time with Liz, who was superb in dull gold, but there had been no attempt to hide the special smile, or her sparkling response.

After an hour or so Tamsyn decided that this must be quite the worst evening she had ever endured. John had spent much of his time circulating; she found herself observing him with a coolly dispassionate glance, and what she saw appalled her. He looked like every cliché she had ever heard about the rising young executive; smooth, polished, always polite and smiling, too eager with a cigarette lighter and a smile which was a little too ready. And always his eyes shifted and moved, as though he was searching for someone of greater importance to talk to.

Shame of her fickleness overcame her. Set at nought was her love, an anaemic thing against the violent upsurge of emotion which gripped her whenever she thought of Grant, yet she had thought it real and true. With ghastly clarity she faced the bitter fact that she had been dazzled by a handsome face and a masterful manner, the classic situation of the secretary who falls in love with her boss. It had taken the infinitely more primitive attraction she felt for Grant to make her see her hero-worship of John for what it really was—propinquity, her own naïveness, and a measure of physical attraction.

At one end of the big room potted plants had been arranged to form a kind of arbour; Tamsyn found a seat there and sank down gratefully into it, her head throbbing, her mouth dry. A band of islanders were playing guitars softly, their mellow voices harmonising in a selection of middle-of-the-road melodies, all of them touched by the haunting rhythm of Polynesia. Above the music the voices rose and fell, a pleasant hum of conversation and laughter, which alienated her.

For what seemed a long time she sat there, wondering whether she would fall out of love with Grant just as she had with John. In a way she hoped that she would, for then the pain in her breast would go away; unfortunately something as primitive as the emotions which had been wakened by his dark attraction warned her that it was not going to be as easy as that. Somehow Grant had found the key to her heart, and while she might love again it would never be as wholeheartedly, as shamelessly as she did now.

So, she told herself, it's an experience. If he doesn't love you at least you've had the privilege of loving him. It can't hurt for ever.

She stood up, squaring her shoulders in a brave call on her courage, and moved out from the protection of the greenery.

And into John's arms. 'Darling, I was coming to look for you,' he exclaimed, frowning slightly. 'Don't tell me you have a headache!'

'No.' She forced a smile. 'I just wanted to rest a little.'

His brow cleared. 'A bit shy, I suppose, and I've neglected you shamefully. Never mind, love. They're dancing next door. Let's go and join them.'

At least she did not have to talk while they danced. Soon one of the engineering staff cut in and made her laugh, and then another and another, as though they were in a conspiracy to keep her on her feet all the time. After a while she lost any desire to hide away and floated in their arms, a tall, slender swaying thing, graceful as a lily, her head poised proudly on her neck, green eyes slumbrous with secrets, while she made the conversation expected of such occasions.

At last someone touched her on the arm and she paled a little, but laughed as she said goodbye to the youngest engineer of them all and was swung into Grant's arms.

For a while they danced in silence, then as the tension seeped out of her and she became suddenly thrillingly alive, he said, 'Ready to go?'

'Why—yes.'

'Saunders is quite happy for you to come home with us, and we're ready to go now.'

'I see.' She looked no higher than his shoulder, saw John dancing with the wife of one of the island officials and said quietly, 'I'll get my things.'

'We'll finish this first.'

Sheer heaven to be held against him while the guitars sang a Polynesian love song softly and throbbingly! Tamsyn schooled her expression into one of polite indifference in case anyone should be watching, but a shiver touched her skin as she met Liz Holland's gaze across the room and read there hatred and anger which seared into her soul.

'Cold?'

'No,' she said swiftly, wondering with a sick feeling in the pit of her stomach just what Liz had seen to cause such a violent reaction. Tamsyn was certain that nothing could have been read from her face; she had set too close a guard over it, and a fleeting glance up at Grant showed his features set in a mask of polite hauteur from which nothing could be deduced. Surely Liz was not so pathologically jealous that she could not bear the sight of Grant dancing with anyone else!

The music slowed, stopped, there was some polite clapping, and then Grant's hand at her elbow, steering her towards the side of the room. The goodbyes were wearisome to a suddenly exhausted Tamsyn; she wished only to be in her bed, alone with her misery.

John escorted her to the car, but there was no chance for

any private conversation; indeed, he seemed more interested in Madame than in his fiancée. Tamsyn found it hard to believe that she had ever thought love existed between them.

The ride home was made in comparative quietness. Madame and Monsieur de la Tour talked softly in the back, but Grant said nothing, beyond a cursory enquiry about Tamsyn's comfort before concentrating on the road. Apparently the Gascoigne family were coming home in the other car driven by the chauffeur, Grant preferred to drive himself.

Once back, there was wine and then the blessed relief of solitude in her own room. Tamsyn looked around, smiling slightly. It had become like home, a place of refuge.

A knock at the door made her frown. Surely not Solange, ready to discuss the evening. Any comments, and she, Tamsyn Forsythe, would scream! Solange's dark eyes saw too much as it was; after her uninhibited references to her own fiancé it would be humiliating to hear her discuss the lukewarm attitude John had displayed and she had reciprocated.

But when she opened the door it was to find Grant there, holding the bag she had left in the salon. It looked ludicrous in his hand, a silver frippery of a thing dwarfed by his lean strong fingers.

'Oh—thank you,' she said inadequately.

'My pleasure,' he returned with sardonic emphasis, grey eyes too intent as they scarred her face. 'You look a little *triste*, as Solange would say. Missing your usual goodnight kiss?'

'Yes!' she snapped, turning back into her room.

'Tut, tut. Perhaps I'd better offer a substitute as it was I who dragged you away.'

'Don't——'

But she was too late. His mouth bruised hers into silence.

'Not as gentle as your man, but I can assure you that there's considerably more feeling than he gives you,' he said harshly.

One hand to her mouth, Tamsyn looked at him, tears slowly forming in her eyes. Grant put out a finger and touched her cheek, not ungently.

'Go to bed, baby,' he advised cruelly. 'You have a lot of growing up to do before you're fit to marry anyone, even so anaemic a character as your John.'

'I hate you,' she whispered.

'If I believed that, I'd rejoice,' he returned enigmatically, his expression as inflexible as a bird of prey. 'What shall I bring you back from the States?'

'Yourself,' she said, but she said it silently, lashes lowered to hide the naked yearning she knew was in her eyes. Out loud she said stonily, 'I don't accept presents from strange men.'

'Only their kisses,' he commented coolly. 'And don't shake your head at me, Tamsyn. You enjoy my kisses as much as I do. Admit it to yourself and who knows, things may begin to straighten themselves out.'

'It means nothing.'

He laughed and scooped her against his side, as casually as if he had every right to do it. 'Does this mean nothing?' he demanded, his hand over the spot where her heart seemed to be leaping from her body. 'Or this?' touching his lips to the hollow of her throat where another betraying pulse fluttered. 'Your breath is coming too swiftly through your lips to be natural, and the colour in your cheeks isn't natural either, *mignonne*. Face facts, Tamsyn. Only facts can make you free.'

'What facts?' she asked bitterly, sick at heart. 'That

there's something between us? I know that. I don't have to like being subject to a kind of madness of the senses, and I don't have to give in to it and lose what little self-respect I've retained. Why won't you leave me alone?'

'I'll let you discover why,' he said coolly, releasing her. 'Off you go to bed, my child. Be kind to Grand'mère when I'm gone, won't you, and don't work too hard.'

The paternal, mocking note in his voice made her colour angrily, but she contented herself with a flashing look of anger. In a war of words he had all the weapons, for he was invulnerable to attack and she was only too easily wounded.

'I'll see you in a week or so,' he finished. 'I have to call in at Sydney on my way home.'

Tamsyn looked up, endeavouring to hide her sudden astonishment with just the right amount of casual interest. 'Sydney?' she echoed.

'Yes.' His eyes gleamed with mockery. 'A bustling city, Sydney. The headquarters of quite a few firms, Smythe, Smythe & Sons being one of them. I'll be calling in to see them.'

'Why are you telling me this?'

The smile which pulled at his mouth was cruel, almost predatory. With a sick feeling in the pit of her stomach Tamsyn realised that he enjoyed hurting her, and that he had no illusions about her interest in his dealings with their biggest rival.

'I thought you'd be interested, *chérie*,' he said smoothly. 'Goodnight.'

CHAPTER EIGHT

'He said *what*!'

Tamsyn licked her lips. 'He said he was going to see Smythe, Smythe & Sons.'

John had actually gone pale beneath his tan. The hotel room was very quiet except for the faint hum of the air-conditioner and the mellow voice of someone singing a sad love song in the garden below. John stared at her, his hands stilled around a wad of papers which he had been putting into order.

'He didn't say why?' he demanded sharply.

'No.'

John closed his eyes as if in anguish. 'Didn't it occur to you to ask him the reason?' he said clearly, spacing the words as though he was speaking to someone extremely short on intelligence.

A faint flush touched her cheeks. Wondering rather feverishly just what he would say if she blurted out the events which had led up to Grant's statement, she shook her head. 'If he'd wanted me to know, he would have told me.'

'Of course, you know him so well,' John said sharply. 'Damn it, Tamsyn, the whole reason you're out there is to find out which way he's going to jump! He gave you the perfect opening and you didn't take it up! What the hell is the matter with you?'

'I couldn't ask him baldly if he was going to give the contract to Smythe's,' she retorted defensively, angry in her turn.

'I didn't expect you to. Couldn't you have used a bit of tact, and got it out of him without actually questioning

136

him?' He ran his hands through his hair, his eyes very bright and hard as they rested on her face. 'Honestly, Tamsyn, you're a bigger fool than I thought! The man is hot for you—why didn't you trade him a kiss for the information?'

'John!' Shock drove the blood from her face, leaving her paper-white and shaking. All of a sudden this man was a complete stranger—and yet she did not find herself unable to recognise him! Perhaps, all along, she had known that he was capable of this.

He laughed mirthlessly. 'Don't act the innocent, my dear. I didn't say go to bed with him, after all. And it's not as though he hasn't kissed you before! But at least you made the most of that and got some very pertinent information in return for the lapse. Perhaps,' he said crudely, 'if you'd made yourself available we might have got the contract.'

Very carefully Tamsyn put the file she was holding back on the table. In spite of the fact that she had had some time to get used to the idea of not marrying John, it hurt to think that the man she had fallen in love with had been a complete figment of her imagination. His diamond seemed to weigh her hand down. Slowly she slid the smooth, heavy thing from her finger and held it out to him.

'You'd better have this back,' she said tiredly. 'I'm sorry.'

He made no attempt to take it. 'You don't have to, you know,' he remarked conversationally, stuffing his hands into his pockets as he leant back against the desk.

Tamsyn shook her head, aware of the watchfulness of his glance. 'I'm sorry,' she repeated, and put the ring down on a small table.

'I don't think you are, really. Do you think you can persuade him to marry you?'

She looked up sharply. He was smiling, almost as though he was enjoying this. 'I doubt it,' she said simply.

His eyebrows lifted. 'And so?'

'Nothing.'

After a moment he straightened up and said persuasively, 'Look, love, there's no need to get yourself in a twist just because you don't like my methods. Your own aren't so lily-white when you consider them. I don't know how far things have gone between you and Chapman, but I'll bet there's been more than a bit of a kiss and cuddle by a waterfall, and yet you haven't done anything about breaking off our engagement till now. Almost as though you want to eat your cake and have it too. If I'm not complaining why should you?'

Very quietly Tamsyn asked, 'Do you really mean that? It wouldn't have worried you how I behaved provided I'd made sure of the contract?'

He flushed at that, but shrugged. 'I don't know that I'd go that far, exactly, but I can't say that I'd break my heart over a few kisses. The attraction was obvious—that first night you both looked as if you'd caught fire from each other. If you'd used your head—! Only you had to fall for the guy.'

'Grant isn't the man to be content with a few kisses,' Tamsyn said quietly. 'Didn't that occur to you, John?'

He shrugged again. 'He's enough of a gentleman not to force you, and you—well, let's face it, sweetie, you are a cool thing, aren't you?'

'Frigid?'

'Don't look for insults. Cool, I said, and that's what I meant. I happen to like my ladies that way.'

Because they posed no threat, offered no competition to his real love, business. Some of Tamsyn's anger and disillusionment faded away. She could not think of him as wholly vicious, plotting to use the flare of attraction between Grant and her to further his own ends; he certainly had manoeuvred so that whatever happened would be to his advantage, but he had meant her to come to no harm. Perhaps, in his own way, he loved her, if he could love anyone other than himself. Perhaps, if he didn't marry for purely sensible reasons, he would one day meet the woman who would knock him completely sideways and turn him into a normal man, with all of the jealousy and despair and hunger that were part of love.

'I'll get these done as soon as I can,' she said at last, picking up the file.

He nodded. 'OK. Good luck with your manhunt, but don't get your hopes too high, will you? The luscious Liz seems to have everything under control in that department. You're quite sure he gave you no inkling at all about the reason for his visit to Smythe & Smythe?'

'None at all.'

'OK. We'll work on the assumption that he's accepted their findings, and see what we can do to counter them.' He looked at her and said more gently, 'I'm sorry, Tamsyn. I guess what we had wasn't strong enough to stand against whatever it is that Chapman has for you. I've had a while to live with the idea. That night you met him—it stuck out a mile that there was something pretty potent there. The old girl felt it too; that's why she asked you to stay with them, I think. So that she could keep an eye on you. It suited me right down to the ground, of course.'

'John, I——'

'Forget it,' he snapped. 'We could have made a go of it, you and I; we have a lot in common, but I should have waited until after you'd had a passionate affair.' His voice

assumed an experienced note as he went on, 'You might as
well have it with him. It will get those romantic yearnings
out of your system and he'll probably treat you so badly
you'll want nothing more than a marriage based on all of
the things that passion tosses out of the window—liking
and compatibility, similar tastes and interests. You and he
have nothing in common, you know.'

Tamsyn bit her lip; if John continued in this sophisticated, tolerant way she was going to hit him over the head
with the nearest ashtray! The fact that he knew about her
feelings for Grant seemed to smirch them; his advice she
found insulting and degrading, but it would be silly to
antagonise him by saying so, and sillier to let him see the
relief she felt at the ending of their engagement.

'Do you want me to stay here? As your secretary, I
mean,' she asked, picking up her handbag.

'Good lord, yes.' He seemed genuinely astonished at the
question.

She could not resist the temptation to murmur, 'You
seem convinced of my loyalty—in that respect, at least.'

'I am.' He looked at her, and said softly, 'It's been fairly
obvious to me that you've had one hell of a time, sweetie,
lashing yourself into misery because you're too scrupulous
for your own good. I know damned well that Grant Chapman would never get any secrets about McHale's from you,
whatever methods he used. And really, Tamsyn, he doesn't
need to, does he? He'll know it all as soon as we submit our
figures.'

'Yes, of course.' For a moment she hesitated, thinking
how fitting it was that their engagement should end in this
almost friendly, businesslike way. It had been a fairly cool
affair the whole way through, a kind of extension of their

relationship in the office, and the ending of it affected neither of them very much. John would, no doubt, find a new fiancée just as easily as he'd find a new secretary, and both would be very good at their job, and John would go on fighting his way up to his vision of personal power, untrammelled by the exigencies of emotion. Whatever happened, Grant had saved her from that half-life, had made her aware, as she had never been before, of herself as a human being with intense needs and desires. In the future such needs and desires might have to be sublimated, but she was no longer in danger of repressing them completely. Better to suffer and live than merely exist in comfortable dullness!

The thought made her smile in irony, but John was already scooping up the ring, and did not notice. He would not have liked it, for he had his share of pride, and it had taken more of a beating than he was prepared to admit.

As she turned to go he said casually, 'Good luck. I'll ring tomorrow to see how things are going.'

Work was not exactly a panacea for all of her ills, but at least it gave her mind something to do other than conjure up visions of a darkly handsome face and eyes which could be cold as Arctic seas or burn with leashed passion.

Tamsyn attacked the pile of papers with determination, ignoring the siren call of sunlight and exotic scents. The house seemed incredibly empty, but Madame made no effort to fill the gap left by Grant and the Gascoigne cousins.

'I am in need of a rest,' she remarked after dinner, leaning back in the high-backed chair.

Tamsyn looked rather anxiously at her. There were cer-

tainly shadows beneath the dark eyes, and was that an in-
cipient tremble in the beringed fingers as they curled
around the tiny coffee cup?

The heavy lids opened, transfixing Tamsyn with that
cynical, humorous glance which seemed to understand so
much.

'Do not look so perturbed, my child,' Madam said drily.
'I am old. Naturally I rest more. And as Grant brings back
some friends, so I must be alert. These Americans—they
like to be doing something all of the time. When I was
young it was not considered fashionable for young women
to display such energy, but times change, and I with them,
I hope. They are pleasant, very friendly and open. You will
like them, and they will find you fascinating with your reserve and good breeding.'

Tamsyn flushed, her expression vividly revealing her
astonishment and a certain shy pleasure. Smiling gently,
Madame touched the slender, ringless hand on the arm of
the chair next to hers.

'You are surprised that I speak so? I do not know why,
my child. I have never been a snob, to judge people by their
ancestors. My own bore many titles, but were descended
from a brigand whose vices were repeated many times down
the centuries. Genealogies are interesting, but should not be
sacrosanct.'

To which there was no answer. Acutely aware that the
shrewd eyes had noted the pale band on her finger where
John's diamond had rested, Tamsyn wondered rather desperately whether she should say something about the ter-
mination of the engagement, but could think of no way of
approaching the subject with *savoir faire*.

After a few seconds the deep old voice went on, em-
broidering on the subject of genealogies as the islanders

understood them, and the awkwardness passed. In the subsequent days Madame made no mention of that naked-looking finger, or the reason for it. Nor did she comment on the fact that her guest was working long hours over the typewriter, exhausting herself with reports and letters and the mass of stuff which John sent out by car each day.

Things were hotting up. As she typed and sorted and re-arranged Tamsyn could not help but be impressed by the work which had been done, the thought and care which had gone into the survey. The hand of the anthropologist could be seen in several amendments and a subtle but definite change in the aims and objects of the study. It was, she thought, a very responsible effort, and given a modicum of luck, provided a blueprint for development which could give the islanders an increasingly affluent standard of living without disrupting their present life style too much. Surely none of the other firms, not even Smythe, Smythe & Sons, could have produced anything better!

Yet Grant was going to see them in Sydney. Which must mean something, though probably not that he had decided to lend the weight of his support to them; Tamsyn thought she knew him a little better than John, and she was almost convinced that he would not make up his mind one way or another until he had had a chance to study all of the details. He was a just man; he was also no fool, and certainly his sincerity where the island was concerned could not be queried. He really loved Fala'isi and knew himself to be an islander in spite of his frequent trips overseas and a wider and more sophisticated way of life than the island could offer.

It was useless to puzzle her brains for the reason why he told her of his plans to visit Sydney. When he wished, he could be as enigmatic as the Sphinx. It had amused him to toss the information at her. Perhaps, she thought bitterly, that had been the sole reason for it; a cruel desire to see the fear and anxiety it caused her.

But even as she thought it she knew she was being unfair. Though capable of cruelty, he was not a cruel man, and she was almost convinced that he had such control of himself that nothing was ever said or done by him without a very good reason.

Her hands stroked the rough trunk of a coconut palm. Very soon all of this would be nothing but a memory of pain and an ecstasy she could never hope to experience again, yet she was glad in spite of everything that she had come to Fala'isi. Perhaps one did not miss what one had never experienced, but she knew now that even when she had thought herself happy with John there had always been an unrecognised query in the back of her mind. Perhaps, had they married, she would have felt that query grow into emptiness and eventually recognised it for what it was, the realisation that affection and a certain physical attraction is no substitute for love. And perhaps she would have sublimated that craving for true closeness with good works and charities and her children as so many women she knew seemed to.

At least there was no longer any likelihood of that sort of life. In a way Grant had made her grow up, forcing her into adulthood. She had learnt so much from him. She had not known that a man could tremble with passion, or that his mouth could bruise and yet promise ecstasy at the same time; she had not even known, she thought despairingly, that there could be an attraction between two people so strong that it almost overrode all considerations of honour. And she had not known that the temptation to surrender to desire could be overmasteringly sweet yet frightening in its intensity. That he had enough self-control not to persuade her into something she would bitterly regret later was yet another thing to admire in him.

Sighing, she turned back towards the garden, wondering bleakly whether she should accept the adage that half a loaf is better than no bread, but knowing that she could never bear to be remembered by him only as a mistress. When one loved, one's needs were so much greater. Although she had not been able to hide the fact that she wanted him, she could retain pride and a little dignity by refusing to allow herself to be coupled with the other women who had sated his physical needs and then been discarded.

It was then that she knew that she must go back to New Zealand before Grant came back.

The realisation had lain in the back of her mind since the moment she had slid the engagement ring from her finger and given it back to John, but she had refused to accept it. Now, bleakly, it had to be faced, for without the protection that that diamond had afforded her Grant would not be constrained and the next time he kissed her might be her undoing. Naïve she might be, but she knew that the ring had in a way prevented both of them from revealing the full depths of their passion. If it flared once more, how could she refuse him when she so ardently wanted to experience the rapture which he could give her?

A quite incredibly large scarlet and gold butterfly flapped its way slowly between the palms, heading towards the garden. Tamsyn became aware that her hand was clenched tightly against her mouth, that her heart was thudding with frightening force in her breast.

Taking a deep breath, she set off to follow the scarlet lure. If the memory of his lovemaking could have such an effect on her she could not put her self-discipline to any sort of test. She must get away and that meant leaving before the end of the week, as he was returning with his party of American friends on Monday.

With despairing efficiency she made plans as she walked beneath the feathery fronds of the palms. Once—a short time ago measured in days, aeons if one went by heartbeats—she would have been entranced by the South Seas enchantment, the perfume of the white ginger which was stealing on the soft breeze, the soft hush of the palms in the breeze, even the green and black spider scuttling down the nearest trunk. Now all her senses were tuned to the sight of a tall dark man with blue lights in his hair and a smile which tore the heart from her breast.

Such desolation flooded her being that she almost decided then and there to stay and take her chances. After all, she thought cynically, he could hardly seduce her with a house full of Americans in residence, especially if the women behaved typically and swarmed around him like moths around a candle. It would be agony to see him charming them all with that arrogant courtesy, but it would be preferable to leaving him.

Perhaps the tension between heart and head would have continued until it was too late for her to run back to the safety and security of her family. Looking back, Tamsyn could never decide what she would have done had she not been pushed into a decision that afternoon. It was unbearably hot. The swimming pool beckoned, but even the coolness of the water and the beauty of the little Greek folly could not prevent her mind from racing around in circles.

The trouble was, she brooded, that Grant knew women only too well, and she—well, she had had experience only of ordinary men, not subtle, complex creatures like Grant Chapman, who had pitted his wits against some of the cleverest business brains in the world and come out on top. If he had deliberately set out to confuse and bewilder her he could not have made a better job of it, but she was certain that he had not deliberately tried to break up her relationship with John. That first night they had met, she had felt what she had thought then was antagonism; with his greater knowledge of the war between the sexes he had recognised it instantly for the attraction it was and she was rather afraid that he had exploited it merely because he was a man and she had been available.

But at that thought she shook her head fiercely. That was not Grant, not casual lust, casually surrendered to, because he was a man and she a woman. Beneath the surface there had to be some reason for his lovemaking; the only one which fitted the facts was his interest in using her to find out just what sort of man he had to deal with in John. If that was so, she thought, back on the see-saw, then the sooner she left Fala'isi the better.

Wearily she climbed from the pool, walking swiftly across the sun-bright tiles towards the coolness of the little temple. She had tanned since coming into the tropics, but the sun was still too hot to bear for any length of time on wet skin.

'You look a little sad. Are you missing someone?'

Liz Holland was standing beneath the pergola, elegant in a dress the colour of crushed raspberries, her beautiful face as coolly remote as a star. 'I'm sorry if I startled you,' she drawled, when Tamsyn jumped at the sound of her voice, 'but I did want to see you alone.' She gestured towards the chairs in the shade of the vines. 'Let's sit down, shall we? I won't take up much of your time, but what I have to say is important, although I'm afraid it won't make pleasant listening.'

The dark eyes glittered in an unnerving way which warned Tamsyn more clearly than words could have done that Liz was in no mood to be put off. She looked almost demented, Tamsyn thought uneasily as she sat down, pulling her towelling robe closely about her.

But the other girl seemed in no hurry to begin. Long red fingernails tapped on the paper she was carrying; without haste she pulled sunglasses on and sat back in the lounger, before handing the paper across to Tamsyn.

'Read it,' she said, adding with elaborate unconcern, 'You have to hand it to the Americans, they're very quick off the mark.'

It was an American newspaper. A swift glance at the top of the page revealed that it was published on the west coast, and that it had been printed two days before.

'I've ringed the relevant portion,' Liz said harshly.

It was a photograph of Grant, elegant in dinner jacket, apparently taken at a gala evening of some sort, for the girl who clung to his arm wore full evening regalia, as shown by the plunging neckline of her dress and the sparkling drops which glittered in her ears. She was very beautiful, and she was gazing up at Grant with adoration.

Tamsyn felt as though she had been kicked in the stomach. A wave of nausea gripped her, then passed over. Very carefully she read the caption. 'Lovely Sue-Ellen Van Humpe, daughter of Julius Van Humpe, well-known merchant and philanthropist of San Francisco, was escorted to the opening of the Olympic Theatre last night by Grant Chapman of Fala'isi in the South Pacific. Rumour has it that the huge ruby on Sue-Ellen's third finger, left hand, was placed there by the handsome Grant, who has shipping and business interests all around the world. Neither party would confirm the rumour last night, but we think the photograph speaks for itself, and neither Sue-Ellen or Grant denied that they have been seeing a lot of each other recently. We know for certain that Sue-Ellen accompanies Grant when he goes back to his South Seas paradise shortly, so keep your eyes peeled for an announcement.'

A bird called from a nearby tree, *tchong, tchong, tchong*. Tamsyn heard the falling notes as if through cotton wool; she swallowed, and her head cleared, but she kept her lashes lowered. The girl in the photograph looked perfect on Grant's arm; beautiful, sophisticated, and yet even through the grainy newsprint it was easy to see that she was nice.

With a desperate attempt at normality she said, 'She's lovely, isn't she?' A fleeting glance at the figure of the woman beside her showed that she was as still and tense as a coiled spring. Or a cat, waiting to pounce.

A stiff pride she had not known she possessed came to Tamsyn's aid then. She would not allow Liz Holland to see how the gossip paragraph had affected her; it was, she thought defiantly, no business of hers! She could not help a thread of compassion from making itself felt, however. There could be no denying that Liz looked terrible.

Tamsyn decided to brazen it through. Handing the paper back, she said quietly, 'I wonder if it's true.'

'Oh, it's true all right.' The red-tipped fingers clenched in a spasm of anguish, then relaxed into stillness as false as the smile she bestowed on Tamsyn. 'She's perfect for him—rich, not too bright, and she adores him—as you can see from that photo. She'll provide him with children, be a superb hostess and grace the family jewellery, and as she's been brought up very strictly she won't want a divorce after three years, so there'll be no chance of her smirching the honoured Chapman name.'

Liz fairly spat the words, her lovely mouth contorted into a grimace.

Appalled, Tamsyn forgot her own anguish and pain.

'Liz, don't,' she said gently. 'You'll only make yourself ill.'

'It doesn't really matter,' the other girl said desolately. 'Why should you worry?' She made a ghastly attempt at a smile. 'I brought this out to show you so that you wouldn't go getting any ideas. I met your boss yesterday in town. He let it slip that you've broken your engagement and I gathered it was because of Grant. If it was, and I don't blame you for falling for him, the best thing you can do is pick up your skirts and get the hell out of here. Just as I'm going to.'

'I'm leaving for New Zealand very shortly,' Tamsyn said quietly, her mind made up now.

'Wise girl. I wish to God I'd never let myself listen to him.' Liz sprung to her feet, a swift, jerky movement at variance with her normal graceful attitudes. 'My God, he's a swine of a man! If he'd only told me—I wouldn't have minded quite so much—but to go away leaving me thinking that our relationship hadn't changed at all...' She broke off, looking so distraught, her tone so wild and reckless that Tamsyn knew a swift alarm.

'Are you all right?' she asked inanely.

'All right? I suppose so.' Liz choked back an angry sob, making an effort to calm herself. After a deep breath she took off her glasses and rubbed her eyes, her breasts rising and falling sharply as she struggled for control. Tamsyn could see the glitter of tears before the sunglasses were replaced defiantly, as if they were shields against Tamsyn's glance.

'I suppose you guessed that we were lovers,' she said

abruptly. 'Or perhaps you didn't. You're an innocent still in spite of Mr Saunders, and we've been discreet. Grant Chapman has a position to keep up in the island.'

The sneer in her deep voice was clear, bitter resentment and pain in equal parts. 'I didn't care. All I wanted was to be with him. At first I hoped for marriage, but give him his due, he made it quite plain from the first that that wasn't what he had in mind. And after I'd met that old bitch, his grandmother, I knew I didn't have a hope. There's no snob like your poor Continental aristocrat.'

'Madame isn't like that!' Tamsyn flashed, angry at the unmerited accusation.

Liz smiled, a ghastly travesty. 'She's been nice to you because you're no threat to her plans for her adored Grant. With that ring on your finger you were safe. I'll bet you find she's not so affable now you've given it back. She won't try to persuade you to stay on.'

Tamsyn bit her lip, but said nothing more in case she gave herself away. The sun flamed silver on the pool, turning the spray from the fountain into molten gilt. It was getting late, but there was no lessening of the heat yet; it was not until after the brief twilight that there came any coolness into the air. A great distaste for this whole scene welled up within Tamsyn. She felt weary and disillusioned, her love for Grant revealed as a temporary physical infatuation, for how could she love a man who kept a mistress, made love to another woman yet all along had been planning marriage to yet another? It was impossible!

'You'll see,' Liz resumed curtly. 'Mrs Chapman has brought him up to think it's perfectly OK for him to act like an Arab sheik with his harem. I hope that little Sue-Ellen doesn't expect him to remain faithful to her. He'll make her a charming husband—he's a superb lover, and if she's docile she'll never feel the weight of his anger—but he'll reserve himself the right to take a mistress whenever he wants to, and he just won't understand if she finds out and creates about it.'

Tamsyn said softly. 'They may be in love, Liz. I'm sorry, but——'

'I know exactly what you're saying!' Liz bent and picked up the newspaper, then deliberately tore the page across.

'He's incapable of loving anyone,' she said flatly. 'Believe me, I know. That's why I'm getting out. If you've got a yen for him I'd advise you to go back to your nice safe home in New Zealand, patch things up with your nice Mr Saunders and marry him as fast as you can, before Grant decides that a blonde mistress would make a *nice* change from a brunette!'

For a long time after the tap-tap of her high-heeled sandals had died away Tamsyn sat motionless, the westering sun striking flames from her hair. At last when the pain and the anguish had lessened enough for her to move again she picked up the newspaper and the shreds of the gossip page, and made her way back to the silent house.

CHAPTER NINE

ODDLY enough she slept the deep sleep of complete exhaustion and woke the next morning with the slight headachy feeling that usually follows such abandon.

She breakfasted alone on the terrace outside her room, forcing herself to eat the rolls and fruit and drink two cups of coffee. Then, very carefully, she began to make plans to go back home while her every desire yearned to stay here in the freshness of the tropical morning, where the multi-hued parakeets fought in the tree of heaven and fled across the garden like rainbows in motion, and the reef boomed its soft thunder at the very edge of hearing. For all of the heat of noon, the mornings here were fresh and new, and birds sang a dawn chorus at the sun's rising as they did at home, and there was laughter in the house and in the garden just as there was at home. But here everything bore Grant's imprint as strongly as if he were sitting opposite her. At least she would be free of that at home.

But first she must persuade John that she should go, and then Madame must be told.

John was easy enough. 'Yes,' he said simply when she broached the subject. His voice sounded thin and far away at the end of the telephone line. 'We've broken the back of it now, and one of the engineering boys is pretty good with a typewriter, he can take over.' He hesitated, then said with something approaching diffidence, 'What made you change your mind? Have you seen the beautiful Liz?'

Tamsyn frowned. 'Yes, she was out here yesterday.'

'I see.' Another pause, but if he had intended commenting further he changed his mind. 'OK, I'll leave you to deal with the details. When are you going?'

She had already decided this. She would leave Saturday, the day before Grant was back.

'Fine,' came the thin voice when she told him. 'I'll keep you busy until then.'

That left Madame. Tamsyn dreaded those shrewd eyes more than she could say, but when she at last plucked up courage to broach the subject it seemed that things could not have been more simple.

Madame did not probe. 'You are sure you wish to go?' she said.

Tamsyn could not dissemble. 'No, I don't ever want to leave, but by Saturday I'll have finished the work here, and there'll be stuff waiting for me back at the office.'

'I see.' Her hostess sipped coffee, seeming to listen to the impassioned tones of a tenor singing a Verdi aria. Tonight she had felt like the more romantic operas, and Tamsyn had selected a record which combined with the night to create an aura of romance and brooding passion.

'I had thought,' Madame went on serenely, 'that perhaps you might stay a few days after your work here was finished and relax a little. You have worked so hard all this while and really have had no time to enjoy Fala'isi as it should be enjoyed.'

Tamsyn managed a smile. 'I'm a working girl, Madame.'

'A pity. These American friends of Grant's are very pleasant, *très aimable*. A middle-aged couple, the Van Humpes, and their daughter, who is sweet.' Tamsyn watched as her fingers clenched into a fist against the arm of her chair; it took an immense effort of will to straighten them, and she could only hope that Madame had not noticed the tell-tale reaction. When she dared look up it was to see her hostess faintly smiling as the shrewd glance focussed on to a window.

'I see the light-flashers are on their way out,' the deep voice murmured. 'I have never tired after all these years of watching them.'

Because it gave her an excuse to evade that too sharp gaze Tamsyn got up and walked across to the window to stare out at the dancing pattern of sparks on the deep blackness of the sea. She, too, never tired of watching them, and never watched them without remembering that first time she had seen them and Grant had stood beside her, his hand on her arm. If she had known then what pain he was to cause her, would she have fled? Or would she have accepted the pain because of the few brief moments of ecstasy which accompanied it? It was hard to tell, now. All she knew was that in spite of his perfidy she loved him, perhaps would always love him, and he would never know.

'Miss Holland is leaving, I believe.' Madame sounded very faintly amused. 'Did she tell you her plans yesterday?'

So she knew about the meeting by the swimming pool. It was inevitable, of course; the servants were unobtrusive, but they were always there, and someone would have seen Liz either going or coming.

'Yes,' she replied, steadying her voice. 'She said she was going back to England.'

'She intends to work, I believe. It is a good idea. She found life dull here. Grant was kind to her, but that one needs a wider audience to display her talents to. She has no inner resources, and I am afraid that she becomes bored very easily. She will do very well in London, where she can go to restaurants with pop singers and first nights with actors and look sultry and beautiful in the newspaper photographs.'

The serene dismissal in Madame's voice made Tamsyn look at her sharply, suppressing a shiver. Did the older woman not know that Liz loved her grandson—or did she not care? She spoke as though Liz occupied some lower plane of life, some inferior position which prevented her from experiencing the emotions which Madame felt. Could this be an example of what Liz had spoken so bitterly about? 'There's no snob like a poor Continental aristocrat', she had said; Tamsyn wondered whether after all Liz was correct, and the kind if slightly cynical Madame Chapman she knew was merely another figment of her imagination, the result of her inexperience, as the John Saunders she thought she loved had proved to be.

A coldness which owed nothing to the temperature assailed her. It seemed, she thought desolately, that she was to leave Fala'isi with not one of her illusions left intact. Grant was a lecher, Madame perhaps a haughty, heartless old woman, John a complaisant lover willing to sacrifice her honour for material advantage—and she, what of her ideals and attitudes?

The tenor's voice swelled, liquid and golden even in desolation, singing of unrequited love and despair as deep as the ocean. Tamsyn could have wept in sympathy, but pride lifted her chin fractionally. Fala'isi, so beautiful that it hurt sometimes to see such loveliness, might seem to have a blight on it, but she was not going to bawl like a frustrated child for something she could not have. Did not even want, she told herself fiercely. The love of a man such as Grant had shown himself to be was worthless, worth less than nothing in spite of all that he seemed to offer. It seemed incredible that a man who had so much integrity in business and in most of his private life, whose attitudes and outlook she could respect wholeheartedly, clever and a born leader of men, should suffer from such a flaw in his character.

Perhaps it was as Liz said, that he had been encouraged by Madame to believe that he was entitled to pick his favourite for the night like a sultan of old in fabled Constantinople. Part of Tamsyn wanted very much to believe that his upbringing was responsible for his callousness, the other part, the clear, unsentimental part of her brain, told her that even if that was so, he was old enough and certainly possessed the self-discipline to overcome any weaknesses in his upbringing. His actions proved that he thought of women as playthings. Tamsyn knew perfectly well that she could not be content to be treated as a pet by any man, expected to be grateful for the few crumbs of his life he threw to her. The occasions when they had talked, really talked in spite of the crackling awareness between them, came clearly to mind. He had, she thought despairingly, spoiled her for any other man, and yet he had shown her just how ignorant and naïve she was, as wrong over her feelings for him as she had been over John.

No doubt about it, she lacked discrimination, she thought bitterly. With any luck it might come with experience, but she could not prevent a shiver at the thought that there might be no further experience for her. At the moment she could not imagine herself feeling any kind of emotion for a man who was not Grant, and the thought filled her with despair. To love unwisely was bitter, but far more painful would be to find herself unable to love again!

By Thursday she had everything done, completed, and sent back to John, and she was left with a long day to fill in, as Madame had an important meeting on the other side of the island which she could not miss.

'I do not like to go on your last day,' she said, but did not look in the least upset.

Tamsyn felt sadly that Liz Holland had been right all along. Without that ring on her finger Madame viewed her very differently.

'Of course you must go,' she said now, swiftly, in case Madame realised that she was hurt. 'I shall say goodbye to everybody and enjoy the luxury of a day with no work.'

Madame smiled. 'You have bought souvenirs for those at home?'

'Yes.'

'Good. Enjoy your day, Tamsyn. You do not intend to leave the Plantation?'

'No, Madame. I'll have a lazy day.'

'Then I shall see you tonight. Au'voir.'

'Goodbye.'

The house seemed to echo with loneliness around her. Tamsyn swam, tried to read, and came inside to do her packing, found it all done for her and was chased out of the room again by Vatatera.

Servants were fine, but they left a lot of empty hours to fill up. For a while she roamed the gardens, but the colours and scents which had enchanted her had no magic now when her mind and heart were filled with Grant. Even the sun seemed duller because he was not on the island with her. At last, feeling the desire for action strong within her, she made her way to the stables, saddled and bridled Sugar, and set off along the faint trail through the coconut palms where she and Grant had ridden on the day they had gone to the waterfall. His promise to take her up the old road to the temple came to her mind; she decided to go back to look at it before she left the island. Even if she did not go all of the way she could ride up into the hills where it would be cooler.

In the distant past the islanders had lined the road with an avenue of tall, graceful trees of an unknown type with flowers of a peculiar ochre red. Tamsyn wondered if they had been chosen because of this; among the Maoris of New Zealand that brown-red had been a sacred colour. Perhaps it was the same here. She was grateful for their shade, anyway, because it was becoming hotter by the minute as the sun climbed towards noon.

The road had been carefully made, for nowhere was it

too steep to take Sugar. She too seemed to be happier in the cooler air.

Nevertheless, when Tamsyn turned after an hour or so she gasped, for they had climbed far higher than she thought. The temple site could not be much further ahead; far below lay the sea, now wrinkled and green-blue except for a smudge on the horizon which must denote one of Fala'isi's neighbours, low-lying Ruta.

The view was superb, the air so incredibly clear that it seemed she must see the fishermen in the diminutive canoes on the lagoon. Certainly she could pick out the villages along the coast, each round brown roof set on its dazzling white platform, the whole on vivid green grass. And the long sweeping pink beaches, the white building which was the Plantation, the sinuous curves of the roads and tracks and paths, the patchwork quilt of greens which denoted the differing types of cultivation.

Slowly Tamsyn climbed down, passing an affectionate hand down Sugar's neck. The mare was warm, not hot, but in spite of the sound of a stream beyond the avenue of trees Tamsyn decided not to water her just yet. Looping the reins over a dead branch, she watched as the mare bent to crop the short thick grass, then turned and began to walk slowly up the path. Perhaps, if she climbed to the top of the ridge, she might at least see the temple site. A bold spur of the mountain stood out on her left, sharp against the sky. It seemed to be flat-topped, and there, she was sure, would be the ruins of the old *malae*, if one could see them through the thick jungle growth which closed in around the path, making the air still and oppressively hot.

When she reached the top of the ridge it was to find that the trees were too high to be able to see anything through them. Brief disappointment brought a frown to her forehead, but she was too lethargic to feel much emotion.

It was very hot and very still. Even the insects seemed to have decided it was siesta time, for there was none of the usual infuriating buzzing and whining. Slowly she began to descend the hill towards the still grazing mare.

Sugar followed her eagerly to the little stream which formed a pool only a few yards from the old road and drank daintily but not too thirstily. Tamsyn glanced at her watch. There were still too many hours of the day left to fill in. On an impulse she tied the mare up again and sat down on the grass with her back against a tree trunk and her eyes fixed on the seascape below.

She awoke to an immense roll of thunder and the mare's terrified screaming. Dazed, she stumbled to her feet, but there was another peal of thunder, a blinding flash of lightning and then the mare tore herself free and careered like a mad thing down the slope just as the rain came down in torrents, soaking Tamsyn to the skin within the first minute, and chilling her just as quickly.

For a moment she stood bewildered, and then, with a cry, she stumbled to the edge of the old road, looking down it desperately as if searching for a rescuer.

It did not take her long to regain her senses and force herself to think the situation through objectively. Help, she soon realised, was likely to be a long time coming, if ever. No one at the Plantation knew where she was, since she had got Sugar ready by herself, and told no one where she was going. So the first intimation they would have would be Sugar's arrival, riderless, back at the stables, if she could make it in this torrential downpour. What would they do then? Wait for Madame to come back, or organise a rescue on their own? Tamsyn did not know, but common sense told her that she could not stay in rain like this for very long without running the risk of exposure, for up here in the hills the rain had a bite to it and she was clad only in jeans and a cotton blouse, no protection at all.

Fortunately she had a cardigan in a plastic bag. To put it on now would make her no warmer, but if she managed to find shelter, then it could mean the difference between being chilled and coming down with pneumonia, for it was of good New Zealand wool.

But shelter, where could she find shelter? It was useless going off into the jungle looking for it; if once she lost the road she could wander until she died in the trees. And there had been no sign of habitation for an hour's journey down the track.

As she stepped, the water rushing down over the old slabs of stone swept her feet from beneath her; she slipped and would have fallen if it had not been for a branch which hung from one of the trees. Clearly, to go downhill was as unsafe as to leave the track. Her only hope was to continue uphill and hope that the ruined temple would offer some form of shelter.

Tamsyn never could remember much of the struggle to reach the temple site. Before long she was colder than she had ever been in her life, but her will and her stubborn refusal to admit defeat gave her the strength to keep going, the plastic bag clasped protectively to her chest. She had to take her slippery shoes off, and the last mile or so was done with cruel slowness, as her feet were cut and scratched by the rocks. And when the temple did at last come into view she was not comforted, for in the lightning-split gloom it looked old and hostile and forbidding, finding her as alien as she found it.

'I'm sorry,' she muttered, as she passed through the great

stone pillars carved into the semblance of men which guarded it. And she said the same thing as she staggered up the ceremonial way, lined now with statues, and on to the wide white platform which had once held the deepest mysteries of the Polynesian gods.

There had once been a building there, made of stone. Now it was a tumbled heap of stones, but a little way towards the sheer side of the mountain was another, much smaller, which seemed in better repair. Towards it Tamsyn made her way, no longer wincing as her feet were bruised on the stones, only grateful that she had found her way here before the mist which was already veiling the peaks had descended this far.

The second building was in remarkably good repair; it looked, she thought vaguely, as if someone still cared for it. A caretaker, perhaps. In the centre was a fireplace, a round raised platform set with wood and twigs which needed only a match to set them alight.

Lightheaded with fatigue, Tamsyn felt exhaustion ache in her every bone, but she knew that she must light that fire and take off her wet clothes before she could relax. It was rapidly getting darker; the building faced the east, and the only opening was there, a low doorway set beneath the wide overhang. In spite of being stone it reminded Tamsyn of the wooden meeting houses on the *maraes* at home, a sort of stone version of them. The floor was made of smooth slabs, cold to her feet, and in the rapidly falling darkness it felt cold and forlorn and abandoned.

Shivering, with fingers made clumsy by cold and rain, she opened her bag and pulled out the matches she always carried. They were damp, but they struck, and after two or three tries she managed to get the twigs and bark lit, holding her hands out to the grateful warmth as the blaze flared and crackled into life. The building was far too large to be made warm by the fire, but at least she could dry her clothes and keep warm herself.

It was hard work removing her sodden garments, but she managed, and pulled on her cardigan, glad that it had long sleeves, wishing that it came further down her body than the waist. Still, at least she had that to comfort her, and fortunately, her bra and pants would dry almost as quickly as her skin. Thank heaven for modern synthetics, she thought hollowly, making a determined effort to be cheerful in spite of the worrying thoughts which chased their way around her brain.

There seemed no end to the storm. As she draped her jeans over the pile of wood to dry, yet another peal reverberated around the peaks. Now that she was safe and getting warm she hoped that no search party would be sent out until the rain eased off. Not for a moment did she cease feeding the fire. A rapid glance had shown her that the place seemed to be a kind of repository for firewood, although why anyone should go to the bother of carrying it up here she couldn't decide. Unless, she thought wearily, the timber was cut further up the peaks and left here to dry before it was carried to the waiting earth ovens in the villages below. Whatever the reason for its presence she was devoutly thankful. Already she was beginning to feel uncomfortably hot, and from her jeans and shirt rose great clouds of steam.

The flickering light of the fire showed little of the interior of the hut, but it appeared to be perfectly plain stone, apart from the two monolithic carved figures, one on either side of the door, a man and a woman. There was something very old-looking about the statues, as though they had been in the self-same positions from time immemorial, and they did not appear to resent her presence. Perhaps it was her tiredness, but they seemed benign deities, Tamsyn thought sleepily, kind and old as the smiles on their wise stone faces.

Tiredness was washing over her in great waves, but she could not go to sleep, for the fire must be stoked. She dozed, waking with a start as the fire crackled or thunder rolled, feeding the fire and turning her clothes while outside the rain pelted down. Soon she lost count of time. Her watch had stopped and she was asleep when true darkness came, so that she could not gauge her time by the sunset. Snatches of vivid dreams troubled her. She woke once to find tears on her cheeks, and scolded herself for her foolishness. Grant was thousands of miles away, so it was useless dreaming of him, or crying for him, for that matter. He was not hers to weep for, never had been, never would be. Tomorrow she would leave Fala'isi with its deceitful beauty and the savagery beneath its idyllic atmosphere and go back home where she belonged with all of the ordinary, practical New Zealanders. And she would never go where she could see another coconut palm or watch the moonpath over the lagoon again!

Much later the storm seemed to intensify into a fury of such drama that Tamsyn cowered beside the fire, afraid that this was a ten-year hurricane arrived at the wrong season. Common sense told her that this building appeared to have survived all other hurricanes. Fear and exhaustion whispered otherwise. Biting her lips, she stacked wood on to the fire, trying to ignore the wailings of the wind outside and fighting down the bubble of panic which strove for expression within her. She did not hear anything and yet something impelled her to swing round to watch with eyes so dark they seemed black in the flickering light as a stooping man came in through the door.

He looked like a sea animal in his dark, rain-slicked oilskins, but even before he straightened up she knew who it was. Only Grant could make her heart sing into wakefulness, only Grant could set every fibre of her body vibrantly, vividly alive. And though Grant should be in the USA she knew before she saw his face that he was here, with her, halfway up a mountain in Fala'isi.

After one fierce probing glance he ignored her, dumping the pack he bore on to the ground, pulling off the tropical wet weather gear and tossing it into a corner of the hut. Tamsyn stood and watched him, forgetting for a moment that all she had on were bra and pants very scantily covered by a cardigan.

She remembered as soon as he turned his attention to her, and flushing, retreated to where her jeans were still steaming. Wet or not, she would wear them sooner than suffer that scorching glance on her long legs!

'Don't bother,' he said bitingly. 'I've got dry clothes for you in the pack.'

He sounded furious, his voice about as distinct a contrast to the flames in his eyes as could be imagined. Tamsyn's fists clenched at her sides for a moment, but she came over to him, ready to defend herself against his anger.

'How—how did you get here?' she asked, the words stumbling out.

'The same way as you, up the track.'

She flushed angrily, dropping on to her knees beside the big pack. 'I'm sorry I asked.'

'When Sugar came home riderless I saddled Trojan and set off up here. Fortunately she had one of the *'Ipialu* flowers caught in her reins, otherwise I'd not have known where to even start looking.' Each word came clear and harsh, distinct through the wild howling of the wind outside.

Tamsyn looked up, saw him strip off his shirt and blinked nervously. There was no defence against the condemnation in his voice, for she had been criminally careless not to tell anyone where she planned to go.

'How was Sydney?' she asked.

One black brow lifted in ironic astonishment. 'I didn't go.'

What did that mean? Tamsyn kept her head down as she fumbled with the buckle which held the pack closed. 'You —you said you were,' she said after a moment.

'I lied.' He seemed quite unrepentant. 'Did you think I was going to give Smythe's the go-ahead?'

She reacted to the taunt in his voice with anger, made more intense by the fact that she couldn't get the wretched pack undone, and he was standing far too close to her clad only in his trousers, tossing wood on to the fire.

'You intended that I should think just that.'

He broke a length of branch across his knee effortlessly. 'Not you, Tamsyn. I wanted to see what your Mr Saunders thought of it.'

There could be no doubt that he knew about the broken engagement. Madame, probably. Ah, one of the clasps yielded to her fingers. Now for the other.

'Well?' he prompted.

'Well what?'

'Did he consider it your fault? Was that why you called it a day?'

As the other clasp undid, Tamsyn was goaded into saying, 'That has nothing to do with you.'

He laughed, but said only, 'There are towels in there. Pass me one, please.'

Meekly she obeyed the peremptory order and bent her head once more as he towelled himself dry, pulling out the contents of the pack. There were slacks for her and a blouse, a lambswool sweater, but no underclothes. She put them in a little heap to one side and went on tugging. Out came a shirt for him. A sleeping bag and food, a thermos of coffee and a hairbrush, thank God! At the bottom was a long metal tube. Tamsyn pulled it out and surveyed it before recognising it as a flare.

'I assumed that your underclothes were of the usual flimsy sort,' he said from behind her, 'And easily dried, so I didn't have any packed.'

The cool distaste in his voice drew a rasp of temper from her. As she pulled on her slacks she retorted in tones which matched his for contempt, 'Your experience is vast, Mr Chapman, fortunately for us both.'

'That annoys you?' He sounded amused, a hint of the Latin manifesting itself in the tone of his voice. 'I'll have my shirt, please.'

Biting her lip with vexation, Tamsyn sat back on her heels, picked up his shirt and thought better of throwing it at him. In the firelight he looked big and dangerous, his expression hidden from her as he stood with his back to the flickering flames. Like that, a dark silhouette, she could see the lean athlete's figure, the broad shoulders and narrow waist, the long line of legs and the proud, arrogantly poised head. A sudden pang of desire tore at her. Nervously she licked her lips, pushing her emotions down as far as they could go.

It took an immense amount of willpower to get up and take the shirt to that still figure.

He chuckled softly as he shrugged into it.

'You're afraid to answer my question, Tamsyn.'

'It didn't seem necessary,' she said curtly. 'Of course I'm not annoyed. What you've done with your life is no concern of mine.'

'You've made it your concern by commenting on it. Why should the thought of the other women who have impinged on my life anger you?'

This, from the man who had cruelly trifled with women's hearts as though they were cheap toys! Anger pushed out the desolation and need in Tamsyn's heart. Crisply she returned, 'I can assure you that they don't upset me in the least.'

'Then you're more forbearing than I am,' he said astonishingly, from just behind her, and caught her by the upper arm as she prepared to move away.

Like a startled animal she froze, both hands clasped against her breast as if trying to quell the tumult there.

'Because,' he continued calmly, 'I find the idea of Saunders making love to you quite intolerable, and have done from the moment I first set eyes on you.'

'You—you must be mad,' she said, half whispering.

'Mad for you. But you knew that already, so don't pretend astonishment.' Swiftly he turned her, ignoring her resistance. One hand jerked in the tangled dampness of her hair gently pulling her head back so that she was forced to stare upwards into the firelit hauteur of his features. The tumbling words died on her lips as she looked at him. He was smiling.

'You're beautiful,' he said softly, 'yet no more beautiful than many other women. Your skin is like silk and your body has the power to arouse desire, but I've made love to others and forgotten them. I wonder what it is about you that's given me sleepless nights and the first jealousy I've ever felt. You weaken me, Tamsyn, and I don't like it.'

'Quite frankly, neither do I,' she said coldly. 'I think a man of your experience should recognise it for what it is. Lust is a fairly common thing.'

'Common, but strong enough to break your engagement,' he mocked.

Bitterly she returned, 'I hate you!'

He released her, striding across the stone floor to the fire. Over his shoulder he said ironically, 'If I believed that, *mignonne*, everything would be so much easier.'

'I am not your darling,' she said angrily. 'Save your endearments for the enchanting Miss Van Humpe!'

Grant had been feeding the fire with wood, arranging the logs with care and dexterity on the platform, but her words made him look up, his eyes twin diamonds in the light of the flames.

'Who told you about Sue-Ellen?' he asked curtly.

By now she was tired, sick to the point of nausea with the turmoil that his arrival had brought. When the memory of Liz's distraught face flashed across her mind she felt a kinship in their betrayal and knew that she would not give her away. Evasively she said. 'I saw an American newspaper which had a photograph of you both taken in San Francisco.'

'Did you indeed?' With careless grace he stood up and began to heap a pile of fern fronds together. The curtness had faded from his voice. He sounded almost amused as he said,

'You must be hungry. Toss the sleeping bag over here and then get some food inside you. Pour me some coffee.'

'I'm not your kitchenmaid!'

'Oh, for heaven's sake, Tamsyn!' He was angry again

now, dangerously so. 'Look, the last thing I wanted to do after a trip across the Pacific was to run around the mountains looking for an idiot girl who's completely incapable of looking after herself! At the moment I'm teetering on the brink of making violent love to you or beating you; just shut up and do as you're told, will you?'

The grim purpose in his voice told her that he was making no idle threat. Tamsyn told herself wearily that she hated him, but it seemed wiser not to provoke him any further, and meekly she handed over the sleeping bag, forced down a chicken leg and a cup of coffee and didn't dare look at him, intent on preventing him from realising that she was having the greatest difficulty in not provoking his lovemaking and ignoring the morrow.

Outside it seemed that the storm was easing. The rain almost stopped, allowing Grant to stand in the doorway and set off the flare. He watched for several moments, then came back in, remarking, 'They've seen it and sent up an answering one.'

'Who?'

'The other searchers.'

Almost she breathed a sigh of relief. 'Will they be up here soon?'

'No, my darling, now that they know you're safe they'll go back home and wait the storm out.'

His sarcasm brought stinging tears to her eyes, but she dared not wipe them away in case he made some other comment. After a moment's blinking she regained enough control of her voice to say, 'I'm sorry about this fuss, Grant.'

'So am I,' he said chillingly.

Then the rain came down again, and he raised his voice, 'Get into the sleeping bag and get some rest.'

It was a double one, but apparently he didn't intend sharing it. He sat beside the fire, staring moodily into the coffee she had given him. The knowledge that he was there brought a peculiarly painful pleasure to her. For long minutes she lay awake, watching the dark autocratic profile of the man she loved in spite of all his cruelties and faults, and then the day's events overtook her and she slept.

At some stage during the night she woke; the fire was low, but it had been banked expertly, and Grant was lying beside her, his hand at her breast, his breath steady on the back of her head. Smiling, Tamsyn drifted off to sleep again.

CHAPTER TEN

'TAMSYN, wake up!'

Her lips were brushed by a kiss, teasing as a feather. Her eyes flew open and gazed straight into grey ones, cool yet lit by tiny leaping flames. She yawned, and blushed, and tried to struggle away from him, but his arms were firm around her and there was no escape.

Smiling with the mockery which had so much power to hurt, Grant said coolly, 'You're nice to wake up to, which is more than can be said of most of the women I've misspent my nights with. I like my women dewy fresh in the morning.'

'I am not your woman,' she said grittily.

'No?' The amusement faded from his expression, to be replaced by a passion as devouring as it was ruthless. 'You are my woman, body and soul, mine to possess,' he said, his lips hardly moving. 'You fit into my arms as if you were made for them. Your heart beats in time with mine like a twin metronome. That first time our eyes met you felt fear and what you thought was dislike, and I too felt fear, because I'd thought that the sudden *coup de grâce* was not for me. Blood called to blood, and I wanted to send Saunders back to New Zealand. I couldn't do that, so I made sure that you came to the plantation, where I could see you each day and make you fall in love with me.'

Sheer shock robbed her of speech for a few seconds; her mouth formed an O of astonishment and he swooped, crushing it beneath his in a kiss which held passion such as she had never dreamed of.

It lasted ages, until the blood drummed in her ears and she signalled surrender by relaxing against him. Later when she was sane once more, she would regret her weakness, but when his hands moved across the skin of her back, pushing up the fine wool cardigan, undoing the fastenings of her bra, she drowned in a sea of sensuous feelings and could deny him nothing.

'I must love you,' he muttered against her throat, his lips taking as of right that which she no longer wished to deny him.

A shiver ran through her, but he ignored it. With the vivid senses of one who is about to drown she felt the tenseness of his need, smelt the clean man scent of him, thrilled to the faint rasp of stubble against her breasts as he kissed them. She made no protest when he undid the zip of the sleeping bag and gently pulled her cardigan and bra away, though colour flooded her cheeks when he touched her and looked at her.

'So shy?' he said softly, pinning her hands above her head as she made to cover herself. 'What did Saunders teach you?'

'Nothing,' she whispered.

'He must be only half a man,' he said derisively, running a possessive hand from her throat to her navel. '*Mignonne—ma bien-amiée——*' The endearments slipped naturally from his tongue, as if French was his language of love. Tamsyn wondered how many other women had felt his mouth and hands like this, had been roused to a pitch of yearning when the only reality was his strength and desire, the hardness of him and the smooth dampness of his skin beneath her fingers.

Softly, hopelessly, driven by a demon, she whispered, 'I love you.'

He lifted his head, his eyes alight with triumph.

'Will you stay with me—here on Fala'isi?' he demanded. 'Become what Liz never was, my lover?'

He was not lying; it was Liz who had lied, though for heaven alone knew what reason. 'Yes,' she whispered.

'Whatever happens?'

She bit her lip, but could not dissemble.

'Yes,' she said tiredly.

'Even if I get married?'

'Yes.'

There was the triumph of a victorious adversary in his laughter as his possessive glance encompassed the slim whiteness of her body. 'You don't appear to be very happy,' he said softly. 'Is surrender so hard for you, *mon ange*?'

'Grant—I——'

'No second thoughts,' he interrupted, and astounded her by lifting the sleeping bag to cover her nakedness. 'Poor Tamsyn, you've fought such a valiant battle with yourself, and all for nothing. I was determined to bring about your capitulation, the first time my eyes took in your proud head and the mysterious green depths of your eyes. You were a

Sleeping Beauty in spite of that damned diamond, who waited for a man to waken her to life.'

He bent his head, kissed her mouth with slow deliberation, savouring the softness of the lips his own had bruised and murmured, 'We're about to be visited. They won't come in, but if you don't want smiles and knowing looks I suggest you get up now.'

Now that the die was cast Tamsyn felt a lessening of the burden she had been carrying around with her for the past few weeks. The decision had removed one pressure from the many which plagued her; she was not happy, but at least her unhappiness was easier to bear. Somehow she thought she would never be happy again.

One recipe for unhappiness, she thought as she brushed her hair. Fall in love with a man you don't respect, yet be so weak as to agree to be his latest mistress. Dear God, to lose one's independence and self-esteem so easily and completely! To be so much at the mercy of one's body that a man could overset the moral code of one's upbringing just by being! And yet she did not think of John once, or even regret the loss of his protection and his undemanding regard. Not even the realisation of Liz's lie had much power to move her. Life with Grant would be bitter, but there would be moments of great sweetness, and she was tired of fighting his dangerous attraction, too tired to resist any longer.

'What is this place?' she asked suddenly as she began to put things back into the pack. 'I was surprised to find it in such good repair.'

'*Fale aloka*, or the house of love.' Grant shot her a mocking glance. 'In the old days it was the abode of Rangi and Papa, the earth mother and the sky father. Those who wished for fruitful marriages slept here on the first night of their marriage. Some still do.'

Blushing, Tamsyn made a thing of folding the sleeping bag they had shared. From outside came the soft sound of voices, some subdued laughter and the call of a bird, sweet and high in the clear air.

'Come on,' Grant said abruptly. 'They'll have brought the horses up to the palisades. Let's get going.'

Outside it was still very early, but the sun had bounded above an island fresh and renewed as if the storm of the night had swept away all tiredness and age. Fala'isi had never looked more beautiful in its green and blue beauty than it did bathed in golden sunlight, every blade of grass and leaf of tree vibrant and throbbing with life.

Three men were waiting, talking quietly as though raised voices would be sacrilege here. They turned as Tamsyn bent to come through the low doorway and bade her smiling good mornings.

The smiles broadened as Grant followed her. One of the men said something in his own language and chuckled at Grant's reply, his dark eyes resting on Tamsyn's face with twinkling good humour which yet had something knowing in it. Tamsyn felt a flush rising, realising immediately what these men were convinced had happened overnight in the house of love. Basic and earthy as their lovely island, it would not occur to them that two unattached people could spend the night together without pleasuring themselves with each other. They were much stricter where betrothed or married couples were concerned, but no doubt the absence of her engagement ring had been noted, and the fact that Grant had come alone to look for her would be given only one construction by them.

And what had Grant said in reply? Certainly no denial, she thought bitterly, walking beside him across the wide stone slabs and down the ramp between the carved stone figures which had seemed so alien in the storm and tumult of yesterday. Today they looked merely old, a little sad when all around them was so fresh and vivid.

The ride back was like a ride through Eden. In spite of the intense emotional tiredness which enveloped her Tamsyn felt her spirits revive as they went quietly down the path. The sun beat down, drawing up the surplus moisture so that they seemed to be riding through a rolling smoke. The islanders rode in front, mostly silent but occasionally singing one of the old chants which sounded monotonous to Western ears, but not here, on the ancient ceremonial way of their ancestors.

Grant spoke little, did not look at her. It seemed that once he had her surrender he had banished her to some distant part of his brain while he got on with the more important things of life. No doubt this was what her life was to be until he tired of her and sent her back to New Zealand. A corroding bitterness threatened to overcome her; blinking fiercely she concentrated on the path ahead. The horse she rode, a big chestnut, was surefooted and steady; probably chosen just for those qualities, she thought wearily. Suddenly the morning seemed brash in its glittering glory. Her eyelids were weighted with unshed tears and there was an ache in the back of her throat.

'Tired?' Grant asked without expression. 'You'd better have a bath and get to bed when we get home.'

Home! A lovely word, but for her there could be no home any more. New Zealand was lost to her and the plantation could no longer be her substitute.

Odd that she should so implicitly believe Grant when he

denied being Liz's lover. Thinking it over she could not help feeling that all along she had known that Liz was lying. It was just that she had seized on the lie to give her the strength to go home before he came back. Madame was no fool. She would have known, and Tamsyn knew that Madame would not have permitted Grant's mistress free run of the house. She was of a generation which would consider this an insult; Grant, who loved his grandmother, would never have permitted any meeting between her and his latest *chère-amie*. Which meant that as soon as Tamsyn's status as his lover became known to Madame she would cease to acknowledge her existence.

'I can't ...' she said aloud, suddenly panic-stricken at her stupidity.

'You can and you will.' Grant had never looked so implacably determined as he did then, his merciless glance showing her that he knew exactly what she was trying to do. 'You gave me a promise, of your own free will. I'll hold you to it.'

'You had no right ...' she swallowed. She was behaving like a whining child; the contempt in his glance flicked her on the raw.

After a moment he said coolly, 'Just what did Liz tell you? Grand'mère said you looked as though you'd been kicked in the stomach after she left.'

So he had discussed her with Madame. Suddenly she felt exhausted. So many emotions had held her in thrall, she was so bewildered and unhappy that it took all of her will-power to remain upright in the saddle. Trying to hide her fatigue she said tightly, 'Just that you and she had—had been lovers.' There, she had said it without a tremor in her voice.

He nodded, his eyes narrowed. 'Trying to get rid of you,

of course. She knew, right from the start. That would be after you'd broken your engagement.'

'Yes.' Tamsyn could not hide her astonishment.

Grant gave her a twisted smile. 'You don't know me very well yet, do you? If you think I'm such a louse, why do you love me?'

'I don't know,' she said hopelessly.

'Poor child,' he mocked, not unkindly.

The last half hour of the ride passed in a haze of self-reproach and regret. The anguish her foolish promise caused her must have been clear in her face, for when they reached the stable-yard Grant took one look at her, sprang from his saddle and swung her down without ceremony. A moment later and she was caught up in his arms and he strode towards the house.

'Put me down!' she gasped. 'I weigh a ton!'

He laughed softly. 'A fireman's lift would be easier, but I doubt if you'd like to appear in front of my guests in such an undignified position.'

'Your guests?'

'Yes, we arrived back a day ahead—fortunately for you!'

Tamsyn looked angrily into the carved planes of his face, seeing there the evidence of his ruthlessness, and hated him.

'Put me *down*!' she said jerkily. 'Don't you dare carry me in like this!'

He grinned and dropped her on to her feet, but prevented her instinctive retreat by the simple expedient of twining his fingers in her hair and holding her face up to his. A muscle jerked at the side of his mouth as the amusement died from his expression. 'How you despise me,' he said dangerously. 'Yet you love me too. Poor weak Tamsyn, still tearing yourself apart over an unworthy man! Have you no pride?'

The anger faded from her eyes, leaving them glittering with tears. 'Not where you're concerned,' she said brokenly. 'That's what you wanted, isn't it?'

'I'm afraid so,' he admitted without any shame, his finger gently flicking the tears away. A fleeting tenderness softened the hard line of his lips as he bent his head and kissed her eyelids shut. 'Come on, sweetheart, bear up a little longer.'

But she was granted no respite. From behind came a warm American drawl, all longstemmed roses and Cadillacs and laughter.

'So you're back,' the new arrival said, gazing with frank interest at the girl in Grant's arms. 'Honey, you look in better shape than I'd expect from a girl who's just spent the night with Grant. Don't tell me he's losing his grip!'

'Don't embarrass her,' Grant said easily, turning Tamsyn slightly so that her face was averted from the American girl's keen glance. 'She's feeling a little fragile. Tamsyn, this is Sue-Ellen Van Humpe. Sue-Ellen, Tamsyn Forsythe, about whom you've heard so much.'

'I'll say!' The girl's throaty laugh was low and seductive. 'We got here to find everyone in a flat spin over you, Tamsyn. And Grant set off to do his hero-stuff, all grim and worried and black-avised. I said to Lorrie, "Boy, I'm glad I'm not this Tamsyn girl. I'll bet he gives her hell before he kisses her better!"'

Tamsyn looked up at Grant, met the mockery of his glance squarely and accusingly and turned to Sue-Ellen. She was more beautiful than the newspaper photograph had been able to show, she wore an immense ruby on her

engagement finger, and there was not a trace of jealousy in
the wide golden brown eyes as she smiled cheerfully and
quite impartially at both of them. No one could suspect that
she had anything more than affection for Grant, not even a
fiercely jealous woman who loved him to distraction.

'Here's Lorrie now,' Sue-Ellen said, 'He's my very new
fiancé, Tamsyn, and still rather shy about it. Hey—Grant!
Catch her!'

It was the alarm in her voice which was the last thing
Tamsyn heard before vertigo took her in its grip, and when
she recovered the same deep voice was still talking.

'. . . get Madame,' she said swiftly. 'What on earth have
you done to her, Grant, to make her faint like that?'

Grant didn't answer, but when Tamsyn opened her eyes
he bent down over her, his expression drawn and grim. 'I'm
sorry,' he said quietly.

Tears spilled from beneath her lashes. 'Go away,' she
choked, turning her head into the soft material of the
cushions she was resting on. He must have carried her to a
chaise-longue under the tree of heaven while she was unconscious.

'Tamsyn . . .'

'Just leave me alone.'

He took her by the shoulders, his fingers painful on the
soft skin. 'Do you think you can make it to your room?' he
demanded.

She nodded, too spent to answer.

'Right.'

Half carrying her, he took her across the grass and
through the french doors into the cool dimness of her
room, lifted her on to the bed and bent to take her sandals
off. His hands were swift and sure, but stilled after a
moment.

'I can do that,' Tamsyn protested, sitting up.

Grant was looking down at her bruised feet, his narrowed eyes fierce and hard as they swept up the long line of her legs.

'My poor little love,' he said harshly, and sat down and pulled her against him, stroking her hair with hands which were unsteady. 'Are you going to forgive me for being such a brute to you?'

Madame's voice made itself heard, ironic and faintly cynical. 'You would not ask such a question if you had any doubt about the matter, *mon cher*.'

Tamsyn pushed herself away from him, by now completely bewildered; she was hauled back into his possessive grip as he stared over her head.

'Go away, Grand'mère,' he said, without a trace of his usual courtesy.

'I will give you five minutes,' Madame returned. 'No more, so if your explanations take any longer than that they must wait until this child has seen the doctor.'

There was a faint click and they were alone. But even after such an imperative order from his grandmother, Grant appeared in no hurry to speak. He leant his cheek against Tamsyn's forehead and held her for a long moment, while within her breast despair and bitterness turned to a faint hope, one she hardly dared indulge in case it died before it was properly born.

On a sigh he whispered, 'I love you. Do you think you could bear to marry me, my adorable, proud, loyal and thoroughly irritating darling?'

Cautiously she breathed, 'Why? I said I would give you anything you want without bargaining over a wedding ring.'

'I know.' He smoothed a fine fall of hair away from her forehead and kissed her. 'It was cruel of me to make you promise, but I had to be certain that you really did love me. I knew that I'd awoken you to a realisation of what desire is and can be, but I needed to be sure that it wasn't only passion you felt for me. I can be content with nothing less than your wholehearted love, *chérie*, because I love you so much that I don't think I would want to live without you.'

Later, perhaps, she would feel the joy she knew his words must be giving her. Now all that she could do was rest her head against him in a great surge of relief.

'How could my agreeing to become your mistress tell you that I love you?' she asked.

'If these past weeks have taught me anything, they've shown me what sort of a woman you are,' he said roughly. 'Only if you loved me would you consent to such a shameful proposition. I banked on that.'

It made sense, but she had another question to ask. 'Why didn't you tell me then? You deliberately let me believe you were going to marry Miss Van Humpe.'

'Darling, you were lying half naked in my arms.' He bit the lobe of her ear then made a path of kisses down to the vulnerable hollow of her throat. In a thickened voice he continued, 'I had to get you dressed, and the sooner the better. Otherwise I'd have made love to you there and then and not cared a rap about our rescue party outside.'

Her pulses leaped, tingled into awareness as the realisation of what he was saying hit her. Trying to disregard the expert teasing of his mouth, she said objectively, 'I don't believe that. You were completely in control of the situation.'

'Oh—was I?' He laughed and picked up her hand, holding it against the side of his face. 'It's been only your lack of experience which saved you from a fate worse than death every time I touched you,' he said, his eyes fierce and hot in his face. 'If you'd touched me—even once—or responded in any way at all I wouldn't have been able to stop myself.'

She blushed, and made bold by her love linked her hands behind his head. 'I hope my inexperience won't bore you,' she whispered, offering him her heart and soul and body with one quick, adoring smile.

'You'll never bore me,' he said softly, his mouth only fractions of an inch away from hers, his voice flat with certainty and the effort to retain his self-control. 'What I said up there on the mountain was correct. There have been other women just as beautiful as you, but none of them ever made my heart skip and beat or turned my bones to water as you do. No woman has made me so eaten up with jealousy that I let you suffer all the way down the hill just to get a little of my own back.'

'You're a brute,' she said tenderly.

'I know. Do you think you could put up with a lifetime of tyranny?'

She began to smile, but one glance was enough to show her that he was anxious about his answer. The skin seemed stretched over the arrogantly hawk-like bones of his face, and there was something predatory about his mouth, as though he would not accept a refusal with any good grace. If she married him she would be joining her life to that of a man who could be cruel when provoked, who was as ruthless as the pirate he resembled, who would expect far more of her than any less complex, subtle man. Life with Grant would be turbulent, perhaps she would resent his autocratic attitude, gone for ever would be the peacefulness which had seemed her ideal.

But she would not have had it otherwise.

'Of course I can,' she said calmly.

'For a moment I thought you'd changed your mind,' he said savagely.

'I won't ever change my mind.'

'Better not.' His hands found their way around her throat, the lean dark fingers loose yet tense against the silken skin. As his thumbs forced her chin up he continued coolly, 'I would have to kidnap you if you refused to marry me, and that could be a little awkward. I don't think Grand'mère would approve, although she would understand.'

Incredibly enough it seemed that he really meant it! Tamsyn smiled very warmly and lovingly at him and the frightening intensity faded from his gaze.

With a twisted smile he rubbed his thumb along the soft line of her mouth. 'Did I scare you? I'm sorry, my darling, but I'm no John Saunders, to let you go so meekly. In this short time you've twined your way into my heart; if you wanted to go it would bring the whole structure of my life crashing down. Now, kiss me once more, because I can hear that damned doctor making quite unnecessary noises out there in the hall.'

The kiss was brief and tender, then Grant left her to the ministrations of the doctor, a calm middle-aged Australian woman with the tired skin which comes from lack of care in a hot climate. She inspected Tamsyn's cuts and scratches, gave her an injection to combat infection and a pill to help her sleep, then withdrew to leave her alone with her happiness. Within a very few minutes exhaustion overcame her and she slept, a smile on the relaxed curve of her lips.

They both wanted a quiet wedding, but the island conspired against them, as did the gossip columnists of the world so that it ended up as a kind of three-ring circus. But nothing could make Tamsyn nervous now. Wrapped in the warmth of Grant's love, she found it difficult at times to believe that the radiant creature who looked out from the mirror each morning could really be Tamsyn Forsythe.

Because of Madame's age they were to be married at Fala'isi, but Grant took Tamsyn back to New Zealand to ask formally for her hand, and stayed a week on the farm, effortlessly reducing the female part of the family to servitude while the male members agreed that he was a man fit to marry their Tamsyn.

He went back to Fala'isi alone, but within the month Tamsyn flew up to the island with her trousseau and her family and a week later they were married in the little cathedral in Fala'isi, with quantities of Chapman and Forsythe relatives looking on and the islanders giving themselves up with immense enthusiasm to a celebration which threatened to last at least a week.

Tamsyn felt a little divorced from it all. So keyed up was she that everything seemed a little unreal, Grant the only point of stability in the whole day. It seemed hours before she was able to go along to her small bedroom and change with only her mother to help, since she refused the offer of a maid or Solange's desire to help her change. That young lady was more excited than ever over *her* marriage!

They said little, but when Tamsyn was brushing her hair her mother moved across to the window and looked out at the fairyland of twinkling lights which the gardeners had festooned among the trees. Tamsyn got up and joined her. Although the noise of the party could be heard it had been confined to the other end of the house and grounds and here it was quieter. A lovers' moon had risen over the horizon and was flooding the island with light and on the scented air was borne the sound of guitars and singing, as the islanders celebrated.

'It's very beautiful,' Mrs Forsythe said quietly. 'You'll be happy here, and it's not so far away from us.'

Sudden tears made Tamsyn give an inelegant sniff as she bent her head and kissed her mother's cheek. 'You can come and have holidays in the winter with us.'

'Grant has already asked us, and we will.' Her mother's fine eyes were drawn to the emerald which sparkled on Tamsyn's hand above the wedding band Grant had slipped on in the cathedral.

'You're a lucky woman,' she said after a moment, 'but Grant is lucky too. Be very happy, my love.'

They hugged, and then Grant came in. Tamsyn gave him her hand, smiling with all her heart up into the grey eyes where passion and amusement were blended in a measure which brought the breath more rapidly to her lips.

Mrs Forsythe looked wonderingly at his casual clothes, then at Tamsyn's jeans and cotton shirt. 'Where *are* you going for your honeymoon?' she asked.

'About six miles away there's an island, a little speck in the ocean which has just one house on it,' Grant told her. 'That's where we're going.'

They went by fast motor cruiser, one of Grant's fleet, and walked hand in hand up the overgrown crushed coral path to where the house waited, dark on its hill above the lagoon.

'Happy?' Grant asked softly.

'Very.'

He laughed softly. 'Nervous?'

'Very,' she confessed rather ruefully. 'Are you going to make a practice of reading my mind?'

'Your fingers are trembling.'

'Oh.' She felt foolish and said so, adding with a laugh which tried very hard to be nonchalant and succeeded only in sounding young and unsure, 'I thought I was sophisticated, but it appears I'm not.'

'I think that half the trouble is that we really don't know each other very well yet,' he commented quietly. 'Things happened too fast for us to become friends as well as lovers; that's something we'll have to work on. Would you rather I forgo my husbandly rights tonight? You are probably completely exhausted.'

Tamsyn bit her lip and turned towards him, holding her face up. 'Kiss me,' she whispered.

He looked down at her, his features arrogant and predatory in the clear light of the moon, and then tenderness softened his expression and he picked her up and kissed her without haste and carried her in through the door.

When she woke the sun was high in the sky. For a moment she was confused, for the view from the long plate glass doors was completely unfamiliar to her. Just a wide sweep of sea, blue-purple in the sunlight, bordered by coconut palms and a glittering white beach. As remembrance returned she rolled over and looked into Grant's mocking grey gaze. A slow flush of pink touched her cheeks as she saw the glitter of passion chase the mockery away.

'Good morning, Mrs Chapman,' he said.

'Good morning, my husband.'

'Come here.' He reached out a careless arm and drew her down against his bare chest, kissing the top of her head and then the smooth skin of her shoulder. 'Did you enjoy your initiation into the married state?'

She blushed wildly at the remembrance of the complete and uninhibited response he had evoked from her, the piling of sensation upon sensation until she had crashed into a world of sensuous abandon. Their lovemaking had been a wondrous thing, a complete physical and emotional union. Masterful yet gentle, he had given her ecstasy, and in giving he had received it.

So she felt somewhat shy of him, yet closer than they had ever been before, and her laughter had an unmistakable note of yearning in it.

'Very much, but you made sure of that, didn't you?'

'One does one's best,' he said modestly, tracing the contour of her face with a gentle hand. 'By the way, there was something I meant to tell you last night, but forgot.'

'Oh?' She was not really interested, for his hands were working magic on her body, and when she arched against him to kiss his chin he laughed softly and triumphantly.

'Yes, *mignonne*. McHale's got the contract.'

Tamsyn was still. It seemed ages ago that the contract had been the most important thing on her mind. That had been a Tamsyn who had been engaged to John; another woman, almost.

'I'm glad,' she said at last.

'Yes, I thought you would be. The work they submitted was extremely good; we were all very impressed by it. But I think I'd have found something for them to do, even if they failed to win approval for their scheme.'

'Why?'

'Because they brought you here,' he said roughly, pulling her against him as though impatient of the subject. 'God, but I love you—and want you—and need you. And I've never said that before to anyone, *mon ange, ma petite, mignonne* ...'

He began to kiss her, and as her bones turned to water beneath his touch Tamsyn knew that she had found her other half, the man who was her heart's core. A line from some tragic forgotten poet came into her mind: *'Then love came, like the outbursting of a trodden star.'*

So their love had begun, a dramatic nova of emotions which had flamed and enveloped them both in its consuming heat. It would alter and grow, as all true love must, but for the moment she could not conceive of greater happiness. Ahead lay the long years with other joys; now was the time for this freshness of shared passion and love. Tamsyn smiled and gave her lips and her life to her husband.

Best Seller Romances

Romances you have loved

Mills & Boon Best Seller Romances are the love stories that have proved particularly popular with our readers. They really are "back by popular demand." These are the other titles to look out for this month.

A LAND CALLED DESERET
by Janet Dailey

LaRaine had always been spoiled and wilful and selfish — and she had always been able to twist men round her finger! But now she had pushed her luck too far and men didn't seem as ready to indulge her as they once had. Certainly Travis McCrea had no time for her at all. And, as luck would have it, it was with Travis that she had fallen in love!

POSSESSION
by Charlotte Lamb

Laura didn't like and didn't trust Dan Harland, and she couldn't understand why her grandfather thought so highly of him. It was obvious that Dan wanted to take control of the family firm — and her grandfather was actually encouraging him to marry her as a means of doing so. And she was horribly afraid that Dan didn't just want possession of the firm; he wanted her too …

Mills & Boon
the rose of romance

Mills & Boon

Accept 4
Best Selling Romances
Absolutely
FREE

Enjoy the very best of love, romance and intrigue brought to you by Mills & Boon. Every month Mills & Boon very carefully select 3 Romances that have been particularly popular in the past and re-issue them for the benefit of readers who may have missed them first time round. Become a subscriber and you can receive six superb novels every two months, and your personal membership card will entitle you to a whole range of special benefits too: a free newsletter, packed with exclusive book offers, recipes, competitions and your guide to the stars, plus there are other bargain offers and big cash savings.

**AND an Introductory FREE GIFT for YOU.
Turn over the page for details.**

As a special introduction we will send you
FOUR superb and exciting
Best Seller Romances – yours to keep Free
– when you complete and return
this coupon to us.

At the same time we will reserve a
subscription to Mills & Boon Bestseller
Romances for you. Every two months you
will receive the 6 specially selected
Bestseller novels delivered direct to your
door. Postage and packing is always
completely Free. There is no obligation or
commitment – you can cancel your
subscription at any time.

**You have absolutely nothing to lose and a whole world of
romance to gain. Simply fill in and post the coupon today to:-
MILLS & BOON READER SERVICE, FREEPOST,
P.O. BOX 236, CROYDON, SURREY CR9 9EL.**

**Please note:- READERS IN SOUTH AFRICA write to
Mills & Boon Ltd., Postbag X3010,
Randburg 2125, S. Africa.**

FREE BOOKS CERTIFICATE

**To: Mills & Boon Reader Service, FREEPOST, P.O. Box 236,
Croydon, Surrey CR9 9EL.**

Please send me, free and without obligation, four Mills & Boon Bestseller Romances, and reserve a Reader Service Subscription for me. If I decide to subscribe I shall receive, following m
free parcel of books, six new Bestseller Romances every two months for £6.00*, post and pack
ing free. If I decide not to subscribe, I shall write to you within 10 days. The free books are min
to keep in any case. I understand that I may cancel my subscription at any time simply by writin
to you. I am over 18 years of age.
Please write in BLOCK CAPITALS.

Name _____

Address _____

_____

_____

_____ Postcode _____

SEND NO MONEY — TAKE NO RISKS.

Remember, postcodes speed delivery. Offer applies in UK only and is not valid to present subscribers.
Mills & Boon reserve the right to exercise discretion in granting membership. If price
changes are necessary you will be notified. Offer expires 30th June 1985.

EP

* Subject to possible V.A.T.